I0557784

The Silent Whisper

Dr. Dinesh Srivastava

"Flow down, cold rivulet, to the sea,
Thy tribute wave deliver:
No more by thee my steps shall be,
For ever and for ever.
Flow, softly flow, by lawn and lea,
A rivulet and then a river:
Nowhere by thee my steps shall be,
For ever and for ever.
But here will sigh thine alder tree,
And here thine aspen shiver;
And here by thee will hum the bee,
For ever and for ever.
A thousand suns will stream on thee,
A thousand moons will quiver;
But not by thee my steps shall be,
For ever and for ever."

-The Rivulet, Lord Tennyson

The Silent Whisper

Short Stories

DR. DINESH SRIVASTAVA

Anjuman Prakashan

Published By
ANJUMAN PRAKASHAN
942, Mutthiganj, Prayagraj, 211003
Website - anjumanpublication.com
E-Mail - contact@anjumanpublication.com

Copyright © 2019 Anjuman Prakashan
Copyright Text © 2019 Dr. Dinesh Kumar Srivastava

Cover design and Typeset in Anjuman Prakashan

ISBN : 978-93-88556-09-5

The author asserts the moral right to be identified as the author of this work

This collection of short stories is a work of fiction. Names, characters, places, and incidents
are the product of the author's imagination. Any resemblance to actual persons, living or
dead, events, or locales is entirely coincidental.

All rights reserved. No part of this book may be reproduced or transmitted in any form or by
any means, electronic or mechanical, and including photocopying, recording, or by any
information storage and retrieval system, without the written permission of the Publisher,
except where permitted by law.

Dedicated to
My Wife- Mrs. Rekha Srivastava
&
Our Daughter and Son-in-law- Richa Joshi and Suraj Joshi
&
Our Son- Mehul Srivastava

Contents

Foreword

The Silent Whisper is a collection of the most poignant short stories I have ever read. It talks about days long forgotten, buried in the obscure edges of memory. It portrays a rural ambience, now rendered to obscurity but by the magic of the writing it comes alive again, most brilliantly. But rural India is a world by itself, far away, distant from the urban milieu. Rural India has its own rhythm of life where time is measured from the arrival of dawn and ends with night. The heart breaking pain of poverty and yet the most solemn and tireless devotion to the family at the cost of one's health subdues all other hopes; the only hope lingers on- "my children will be better off if I somehow give them education".

Yet the Grandma will miss her grandchildren, as she tenderly counts, in her dreams, the number of mangoes that have fallen on the ground, after a mild storm. She can recount where exactly the mangoes fell, just like the "silent whispers" come over to her, she does not know from where but surely from a faraway land.

Or the silver flute, so brilliantly alive now, dead the next moment as the boy effortlessly takes his last breath, his beloved gone forever. The poignancy is too sharp, the pain turning masochistic yet unbearable joy pervades with a timeless calm. Or the young child taking extreme risk and beating to save a girl from being ravaged. Or the gypsy girl sold by her clan to be a mistress who is left with only talking mynahs to give her company, her lover silenced.

The book most brilliantly describes the power of absolute faith, from "A Leaf of Tulsi" and praying to God not for one's own sake but for the children, grandchildren. And it tells of a goddess who dispenses justice. Or of a tree which travels across continents and a road still left with some trees.

"Silent Whisper" tells you of the canal which cannot speak any more, the urban Juggernaut has taken over, silencing the canal for ever. The birds have flown away, the jackals have been silenced, the water bodies have been filled up, the rain trees and gulmohars have been killed, the wind has died, and "The Last Orchids" have been sold out, their beauty, their symmetry perished by greed.

The agony is best expressed in the "Flowers of Mahua"- the sharp contrast of urban indifference and the tranquillity of the rural setting where nature is at ease with her inhabitants, with millions of stars twinkling in the dark blue dome, as the evening descends.

Driven by the relentless pursuit for the better, far more, for the ever changing personal wish, "The Silent Whisper" is a loud reminder of what we tragically miss out chasing our mirage; the desert will never bloom, birds will never chirp, trees have long died and the peacocks have long gone away; only the sand dunes will play havoc with our mesmerised eyes.

Prof.Bikash Sinha

Kolkata

April 5, 2019

Former Director :
Saha Institute of Nuclear Physics
Variable Energy Cyclotron Centre
Former, Homi Bhabha Chair Professor

Preface

A short story is a focused narrative of a character or an incident or may convey an idea. In many ways it is like a research paper in science, a profession which I have followed for more than four decades. A scientific paper has to be original and its results should be reproducible, by anybody, anywhere and at any time.

This is inherently different and yet similar for a story. Stories deal with people, their aspirations, their anxieties, their fears, their cowardice, their braveries, their weaknesses, their strengths, their ecstasies, their humiliations, their joys, their frustrations, their pains, their sufferings, fulfillment of their dreams, shattering of their dreams, their lack of dreams, their nightmares, their fantasies, their hardships, their failings, their virtues, their victories, their failures, their struggles, their inner thoughts and their hopes. Even though they may allude to events which may have taken place they are not the same as a newspaper report. The latter is not likely to explore their inner thoughts and the effects of the event on the emotional balance of the universe. And it may also not be always reproducible as peoples' actions seldom are, even though they may face similar travails. A story can also record their cowardice for which they hate themselves for the rest of their living moments but which they may never be able to admit; perhaps even to themselves. It celebrates man and his struggles for survival when all odds are stacked against him and when the ground under his feet is crumbling. Sometimes, these struggles result in his complete destruction; but the satisfaction of having faced the adversities is his triumph and we need to celebrate it. And then there are occasions when man wins and exults.

To tell or to read a story is to live through our own pain or the pain of our fellow beings again. Sheikh Sadi once told that:

"Human beings come
From the same source
We are one family.
If a part of the body hurts
All parts contract with pain.
If you are not concerned
With another's sufferings
We shall not call you human."

This statement is considered to be so profound that it is engraved on the hallowed precincts of the head-quarters of the United Nations Organization.

The realization of the pain of our fellow beings carries a seed of change for a better tomorrow. It is generally believed that "to imagine the suffering of our fellow beings and the future of our beleaguered planet provokes rage, dread and an overwhelming sense of helplessness. Rage and dread can morph into an instrument for change, though it is hard not to feel that any change is too little, too late" (Rachel Hadas).

Let me add that most of the stories included in this collection have appeared either in the literary section of The Statesman or its Festival issue. I am grateful to its editorial staff for this kindness. Some of the stories do use the first person narrative, as in **Roots**, to benefit from the power of confession and meditative self-analysis which I had found to be very valuable. And let me add that this is also a silent cry of despair about the helpless of man against powerful odds, which he silently admits. And let us remind ourselves again that this realization should become the rallying point for change.

The stories have been put into an atmosphere which I know well. Even though some of the stories discuss changes in the city of Kolkata where I have lived for close to forty years by now, these are only symptomatic of all cities. Similar deteriorations and changes are happening all over the world. These often have no specific man or woman as a protagonist. These attempt to portray the painful and silent screams of Nature emanating from the agony of its wanton destruction by its own children.

That the world will change with time is understood, but an awareness of the destruction caused by the juggernaut of progresses could help minimize the sufferings which follow.

I agonized a lot before finally including the story "The abode of the goddess" in this collection. It is based on stories I had repeatedly heard from our villagers. I know for sure that stories involving snakes are only an expression of the fear of the unknown. However, the belief of our villagers in spirits which look after all and intervene on behalf of the weak and helpless is a very reassuring and endearing concept, even thoughit may give them only a false (?) sense of reassurance. Thus I have retained it after taking it out several times from the collection. Take it as a fairy tale, if you wish.

I wanted to include one of my short stories where Nature talks of her sufferings. I soon realized that it was extremely depressing and full of despair and took it out from this collection. Instead there are some stories in this collection where trees, animals, and waterbodies are systematically and brutally destroyed by men. If only these trees and animals and water-bodies could speak- their painful screams would have been one of the most heart-rending sounds ever heard on this planet. If the stories included here succeed in transmitting even some of these silent screams, I would consider my job as successful.

I shared some of the early versions of the stories with several of my friends. They were always very supportive and I thank them for their indulgence and their comments which were also used to give the final touches to the stories. I am also very grateful to my mentor **Dr. Bikash Sinha** for very kindly writing the **Foreword** for this collection.

When I approached, **Mr. Venus Kesari**, with a collection of some of my earlier short stories I was pleasantly surprised that he immediately agreed to bring them out as a book. He also suggested to change the name of the collection to **"Roots"**. I received very encouraging comments from my friends and also from people whom I have never known. These events encouraged me to continue to write.

The present collection, "**The Silent Whisper**" is in response to their suggestions. I hope that this is also received kindly by the readers.

While I was finalizing this collection, we lost the husband of my youngest sister, Mr. Pramod Kumar Srivastava. The poem by Lord Tennyson included at the beginning of this book reflects our state of mind at the moment. I was looking forward to making a present of this one to him as he had liked the earlier collection, **Roots,** quite a lot.

I have often been asked how I manage two seemingly mutually exclusive careers- mostly in science and also in literature. Let me add that while science is my main passion and occupation, pursuit of literature has opened an avenue for expressing my feelings. However this would not have been possible, unless my wife took the entire charge of looking after the children, me, and the house. She provided a most conducive atmosphere for me to indulge in my pursuits. I can never thank her enough for the sacrifices she has made and hardships she has endured to make it possible.

My family, especially my wife, our children and our son-in-law have remained a source of joy, support and satisfaction. They have read these stories well before these appeared anywhere. They were also the first critics. However, I have suspected since long that they -being a lot more exposed to world literature have often struggled to find something to like in the stories or to say something nice about these, so as to encourage me. With love and gratitude I dedicate this collection to them.

December 2018   ***Dinesh Srivastava***
                                     C3/44, KendriyaVihar
                               V. I. P. Road, MondalGanthi
                                        Kolkata 700052

1

The Crossings

My father must have been very young when he went to work in the coalmines of West Bengal. I have memories of him coming home, once every year. He normally sent a letter about his arrival, which set things in motion. We would prepare our bullock cart for the long journey to the railway station, for days in advance; cleaning it, oiling its wheels, giving a bath to our bullocks, applying a coat of black soot and mustard oil to their horns, adjusting the belt with the bells to be hung around their necks, repairing the canopy of tarpaulin and spreading a layer of fresh hay in the sitting area. My grandfather used to go to the station with water, buttermilk, 'sattu', 'gur', green chilies, and pickles. I was about four or five years old when I started going with him.

My mother stayed back at home, cleaning the house, the surrounding areas, and the cattle shed. She got a special fragrant clay from the ravine and painted our house. She applied a fresh coat of cow dung mixed with the same clay with water throughout the house and the courtyard and sprinkled water around the house to keep the dust down. And finally, she hung fresh leaves of mango and flowers of marigold tied to a string, above the door of our house. All through this my grandmother sat on a cot, pulling at a 'hookah' and inventing chores for her, and talk of the day when I would grow up and go to work, while my father would retire and look after the fields at home.

The train from Calcutta arrived around noon. I would be very excited and start looking for it, almost an hour before it came. I would jump and look for my father as the compartments went past one by one. Sometimes he would manage to stand near the gate and we would be able to get a glimpse of him before he alighted. He would lift me up in his arms and hold me close to him and I would rejoice in the smell of tobacco, sweat, and coal. Even though tired after a long journey, he would be full of cheer. I never understood then, but I recall that he used to embrace the bullocks and stand still with his eyes closed, for a few minutes before getting on to the cart. I also recall that he used to smell everything that he touched-the canopy, the buttermilk, the pickles, me, my grandfather, and even the water. Was it his way of controlling and hiding his tears?

All through the journey back home, I would sit in his lap, savouring every word that he spoke and replying with a great zeal when he asked me a question. He ate the sattu and drank the buttermilk with a visible satisfaction and happiness. The bullocks trundled along-their bells ringing, while he wished all those whom we met along the dirt road.

I would jump off the bullock cart well before reaching the village and run to our house to announce his arrival, and to tell-how he looked, what he was wearing, and what he had told me, and my grandfather. I would see my mother lapping every word of what I narrated. And her eyes would glow and get moist at the same time when I would tell her that father had asked me about her.

I have already told that my father worked at a coal mine. I remember finding coal dust under his nails, in the folds of his clothes, in his hair, and into his shoes, when he came home. Even the wrinkles on his face held coal dust and it took days of bathing in our river to remove it. During the brief holidays, he went around our fields. I tagged along with him, rejoicing in his company and soaking in his voice.

Sometimes he described his work, leaving out all the details of hardship. Only much later, and that also only once, he had talked to me of the incidents of a sudden collapse of the mine, of a fire starting in the mine, of water gushing into it, and of workers getting trapped there. Only then I had realized that it was a miracle that he was alive.

During these visits he occasionally went to the city, to buy field equipment, to sell grain, or to buy seeds and fertilizer, which was normally done by my grandfather. He took me along with him once. It was to change our lives forever.

On the way to the city, we had to wait with our bullock cart at a level crossing for quite some time. A goods train was to come from Calcutta. As it passed us, we saw wagons after wagons, full of coal. I felt a surge of pride, just watching the wagons and imagining that my father had dug out some of that coal from the interior of earth. And then we saw several trucks parked in the neighbouring mango orchard near which the goods train first slowed down and then stopped. As we watched, a number of people jumped off the trucks, climbed into the wagons, and started unloading the coal. One of them went to the guard of the train and gave him some money. Soon the trucks were full and the train rolled away. I can never forget the rage, the hurt, and the acute sense of betrayal, which flooded my father's eyes. He hardly spoke a word for the rest of journey.

When we returned home, he declared that I was to be sent to school. He added that I was not to work on the field or with the cattle, and that I was not to work at the mines like him, when I was older. Years of working there and the frugal habits of my father had helped us buy some more land and my grandparents were always talking about how by the time I grew up, we would need to hire additional workers. All this changed in one night. My grandmother protested loudly, trying to suggest that my mother must have instigated him, but he shouted her down. I had never seen him in such a rage, before. And I never saw him getting angry again.

He went back to work. After some months, his coalmine was abandoned. He found work at one of the foundries, called Universal Foundry, near Howrah. When he came back he talked of furnaces and molds. He told us of the designs of covers for manholes and storm drains, which the foundry produced and exported all over the world. His letters were more frequent now and he kept a continuous track of my progress.

Some years later, while showing him my books, I realized that his eyesight had started getting weaker. A little enquiry revealed that he and his coworkers worked in very unsafe conditions. But he told me not to worry and to concentrate on my studies.

However, a few months later he lost his job and came back for good. When I went to pick him up from the railway station, I noted that he had a great difficulty in seeing, the corners of his eyes were blazing red, and he was breathing noisily. I took him to a doctor before returning home. He did not argue and went quietly with me. The doctor informed us that several years of working, first in the coalmines where he had sustained minor injuries on a regular basis, and then with the foundry, with the exposure to hot and bright molten iron and steel and the noxious fumes, without proper protection had permanently damaged his eyes and lungs. I saw the look of pity and resignation as he examined him. That look of pity shook me to the core and a volcano of anger and helplessness erupted in my mind.

On the way back, we had to wait at the level crossing again, for a train to pass. The memory of the day when I had waited there with my father flashed across my mind. I looked at him. He was staring blankly at the horizon. I decided then and there, that I would study to be a doctor. I told him of my decision. And he smiled. That was the first time he had smiled after getting off the train. I felt that the smile was a continuation of the rage I had seen in his eyes, several years earlier, when we had seen the coal being loaded off the train.

The storm, which hit our home when I told of my decision upon our return, raged for several days. Only my father's calm assurance helped me keep my resolve. We all knew that we would need to sell our fields, one by one, to support my education; fields for which he had laboured for years under extremely difficult conditions.

Yet it was also the memory of these hardships in the mines and in the foundry, which gave me strength. It gave me courage, when my fellow students humiliated me for my poverty, ridiculed me for my background, and subjected me to insults and physical torture in the name of ragging. I knew that I was being singled out as I was helpless. But every time I thought of giving up, the image of my father, labouring in a dark coalmine deep into the belly of the earth and bent over a tub of molten iron, and now struggling with cancer, steeled my determination. And every time I came home from the hostel, both of us struggled to hide our pains behind smiles.

All this and much more flashed in my mind as I waited at the pedestrian crossing in front of the Duke University in USA on my first day there. I thought of the smile of satisfaction, which had lit my father's face when I had shown him the letter of offer from the University. A day later, he had died in his sleep.

A clinking sound made me look at the road. Along the curve, there was a storm drain and a little further down a manhole cover. And then I saw the markings; 'Universal Foundry, Howrah'. I looked around and saw a row of similar manhole covers glistening in the morning sun and extending to my left and to my right, as far as my eyes, now full of tears could see.

2

The Abode of the Goddess

It was very cold and there was a dense fog. I had missed the train to go to Benaras and was spending the night on the railway platform. The waiting room had no windows. I saw a group of villagers sitting around a fire. I walked up to them. Seeing my city clothes, they got busy and got me a low stool to sit upon. My coming had interrupted their discussion. I requested them to continue. One of them was telling the following extraordinary story. I do not know, whether it was just a story or truth, and I will leave it to you to make your own judgement. I am reporting it in the words of the old man, who must have been more than eighty or perhaps ninety.

The Story of the Old Man

I still remember the day when the vast barren field you see to the north of our village was a dense forest. It started at the edge of our village and continued up to the outskirts of the town. It skirted the town and then went on and on for miles, providing a vast arena to neelgais, wolves, hyenas, hares, jackals, foxes, snakes, birds, and the spirits of the forest. The forest is gone. All the animals are gone. We only rarely hear of the spirits now. I can only pray that they also do not leave us. But there was a time, when one heard of them and even saw them or their manifestations often. And they intervened in our affairs.

Let me tell you of an incident. It took place forty years ago. During those days, if you wanted to go to the town from our village, you had two options. You could walk up to the market and take an 'ekka', a one horse carriage and travel the distance of about twenty kilometers in about an hour and half or more depending on the number of passengers and the state of the health of the horse. The other possibility was to walk through the forest, which was rather dense in parts and you had to cross a river and a ravine. You met people along the trail either going to or coming from the town.

There were also three wells along the route and if you carried your lota (a small vessel) and dori (a very thin rope), you could draw water and quench your thirst. You often met people near these wells, sitting down for a brief rest, and for exchanging news about the prices of food grains and cows and bullocks, about the possibilities of rains, about boys and girls of marriageable age, about herbal medicines, and about court cases. They exchanged stories of wild animals, spirits, and snakes found in the forest, repeating a part of it if new people joined the group and sharing a pinch of tobacco mixed with lime and crushed to a coarse powder on the left palm using the thumb of the right hand before continuing on to their journey. It was always a very good way to know our people.

I was returning from the town. It was a hot summer day and the hot and dehydrating wind, the 'loo' of North India, was blowing across the forest. There was no sound except for the crowing of an occasional crow and the very occasional cry of the mynas, when they spotted any suspicious movement in the undergrowth. Thus I was happy to see two men and a woman sitting under a mango tree near a well. The woman sat on a clean colourful sheet of cloth. A silken shawl covered her shoulders and her head, leaving only a small opening near her face, though her face could not be seen. One of the men had a lota and a dori. I greeted them. And I asked if I could borrow it to draw water from the well. They wished me respectfully and after knowing that I was a Brahmin, one of them rushed to get water for me. They requested me to have a little rest. It was really very hot. I did not mind.

We were exchanging pleasantries, when we heard a huge uproar created by the mynas. Someone remarked that perhaps a snake was on the move. This started a discussion about snakes.

The first person narrated the following incident.

The Story of the First Man

'I was very young then and had come on a leave from the army. I had gone to the town and while returning stopped under this tree to look for ripe mangos which had fallen all around. It had rained a little earlier. There were several anthills over there and they were virtually spewing out streams of winged white ants. Crows, sparrows, and several other birds were feasting on them. This tree was still young then and its trunk was not yet so thick. Then I saw a cobra, coiled around it. It had its hood spread and its forked tongue was lolling at regular intervals, sniffing the air around it. I was well known in the army for my makmanship. I was carrying my father's gun, which was not as good as the rifle to which I was used in the army. Still, I took an aim and shot the cobra. Its hood shattered all over the place. Its body uncoiled and writhed for a while before lying still. It must have been almost eight feet long. Satisfied with my success, I looked around for any other snake and not finding any, went home. A few days later I had to go to the town again. When I reached this place, a cobra rushed out from the undergrowth and attacked me. I was taken aback till I realized that I had my gumboots on and the snake was biting it repeatedly and furiously. My shoes were rather loose. I shook them off my feet and kicked them away, as far away as my strength permitted and fled.'

The Old Man Continued

While we listened in silence and marveled at his lucky escape, the lady moaned, remarking that it was so cruel to kill a snake, in such a casual manner, which was waiting for its mate, and had done no harm.

Then the retired army man told that once a snake has lived to be hundred years old, it grows wings, can fly, and can assume any form. The air stirred by its wings, he told, is so poisonous that it leads to a paralysis of limbs. He also told that such old snakes often have a brilliant 'mani', a very precious stone, which they carry in their mouth and occasionally put it out to look at it, hypnotized. I laughed and added that all of it was a mere superstition and complete nonsense. I saw the lady shake her head as if in pity, at my arrogance and ignorance.

We were silent for some time and then the second person spoke:

The Story of the Second Man

'I am a shepherd. I had brought my sheep and goats for grazing into the forest, some years ago. I climbed this mango tree, to fell some leaves to feed them. I was carrying my shepherd's laggi, a very long and thin pole of bamboo, with a very sharp sickle fixed at one end. While using the sickle to fell leaves, I looked down and saw a pair of cobras, coiled together, and swaying as if engaged in a dance. I was young and reckless. I decided to use the sharp sickle fixed at the end of my laggi, to slice off the hoods of both of them in one quick movement. I succeeded in slicing off the head of one of them. A part of the tail of the second snake was also sliced off. But before I could have another go at the second snake, it got on to the laggi and started moving up to me. I tried to shake if off the laggi, but failed. I got worried and threw the laggi away. I jumped off the tree and fled, leaving my sheep and goats here. Later some friends brought them back home.'

* * *

And the Old Man Continued

We praised his presence of mind and congratulated him on his good fortune. However, the lady broke into a sob and added that such arrogant men have no regard for the life and feelings of other living beings. It was so very wrong to kill a snake when it was mating, she added. Why, why such a wanton killing of innocent animals-she asked, rather pointedly? We kept quiet.

But the man who had narrated this incident, got tense. He was looking at the trunk of the mango tree. I followed his gaze and saw the head of a snake emerge from behind the tree. The snake moved rapidly towards us. Before we could react, it was upon us and attacked first the retired army man and then the shepherd, biting them repeatedly. They fell dead, frothing at their mouths. I jumped away from the spot. However to my great surprise the lady did not move.

Several mynas started a big uproar upon seeing the snake. It slithered away. By then I had recovered my wits and ran after it with a lathi and my unwound turban. I wanted to throw the turban at it to entangle it, and then club it. I threw stones at it so that it was forced to go in a direction where the surface was very smooth and slippery, thus impeding its movement. I gained quickly on it.

Finding itself cornered, the snake turned, coiled itself, and raised its hood, ready to attack. I stopped in my tracks. I thought of picking up a stone to throw at it to chase it away. As I bent, the snake too bent forward, uncoiling as if to move forward. I stood still, now scared. The lady shouted that I should leave it alone. I slowly walked back. The snake slithered away into the undergrowth.

The lady told me that I should have seen the knot in the trunk of the mango tree, caused by the bullet, which was still lodged there. She added that the snake, which had a part of its tail missing, was known to frequent that place and to rest with its head on the knotted trunk.

I looked at the lady. And then I noticed for the first time that she did not cast any shadow! A halo had appeared around her face, which was now partly uncovered. Her shawl had slipped to her shoulders and she was resplendent in her glittering jewelry and fine silk clothes.

I realized that I was seeing the famed Goddess of the forest, Dhamsa Devi. My grandmother had often told me about the Goddess but I had never really believed her. And I realized that I had seen the Goddess presiding over Her Court of Justice and meting out punishments. I also realized that, for whatever reason, the Goddess had wanted me to be a witness to the confessions by the two men and to be a bearer of the news that justice had been done. I folded my hands and bent my head to offer my prayers to her. By the time I looked up She had vanished.

No sightings of the Goddess have been reported since then. But we know that the Goddess still has Her abode there. She still responds to the prayers of weak and innocent and people in trouble. The mango tree with the knot on its trunk survives and people often light oil lamps there. The lamps continue to burn brightly throughout the night even if there is a strong wind. And that confirms that the Goddess has accepted their humble offering.

By the time, the old man finished his story, we could see that stars had started disappearing one by one. He took our leave and got up to go.

It was then that we noticed that he was completely blind.

He walked just a few steps and vanished.

And we recalled that even though we had a roaring fire burning, he had cast no shadows.

3

Revenge of the Gypsy Girl

The plains of Eastern Uttar Pradesh are amazing. You have miles and miles of flat land in all directions, till your eyes meet the horizon, with only occasional trees and mud houses breaking the monotony of the landscape. But then you also have the ravines, not very deep, very serpentine-with stretches of forests of acacia, dhak, and elephant grass, and reed. The flat land empties all the rain water in the ravines, which crisscross the land, and which happily change their course every year-uprooting the trees and swallowing the fields, emptying into small rivers which in turn empty into larger rivers, swelling them beyond recognition, and causing havoc every now and then, during monsoons. These forests are a welcome growth, providing grazing areas for animals, and stalling the erosion of the fertile land.

I was working for the Public Works Department. Our team was asked to conduct a survey of the terrain for building a road-which was to run through the forest, along an ancient trail, from the village of Bholaganj to its neighbouring town about twenty miles away. A small river separated the forest from the village. We camped along a network of ravines feeding into the river. As it was winter, there was no water in the ravines and the river flowed gently, its water crystal clear.

The forest was quite thick in parts. It was full of small wild animals like wolves, jackals, foxes, jungle cats, hares, and neelgais. There were several large water bodies, full of lotus, water lilies, water chestnut, cat's tails, fish, and wild rice. We were happy to note that water hyacinth, the scourge of all water bodies in Asia had not yet reached them, though we knew that once the road was made, the weed would oust the lotus and lilies and choke the lakes.

The river actually skirted the forest, and one of the village songs we heard told that it 'held the forest in its sensuous embrace'. Once in a while we saw a flicker of light in the forest and the villagers told us of robbers living there, who went as far as Lucknow and Agra to commit their acts. They did not bother the villagers and the villagers in turn never told the police about their movements.

They also talked of a ruin in the forest; ruin of a hunting lodge, which was built by Thakur Samarjeet Singh, the grandfather of the present landlord, where no one lived. We had very little time to explore the interior of the forest, where the ruins were rumoured to lay. Even the villagers very rarely, if ever, ventured into the interior, because of a variety of fears.

However, no prodding was necessary for them to tell the story of the life of Samarjeet Singh and his hunting lodge. He was educated in England and was trained to be a barrister. However he went to the High Court at Allahabad, only occasionally. It was mostly to replenish his stock of liquor, and to get his guns repaired. He was fond of hunting and often went to the forests along the borders of Nepal, to hunt tigers, deer, and birds. We had seen several tiger skins in the villa where his grandson lived now, when we were taken there by the villagers to be introduced to him.

Let us get back to the story of Samarjeet Singh. During summer, nomads from as far as Rajasthan came to the village. They camped away from the village, near the edge of the forest. They sold herbal medicines and other jungle-produce to the people. Their women folk went from door to door, dancing, singing, selling charms, and courting men. It was common for the rich farmers to "buy' the nomad women for pleasure-for a week or so, and once paid for, they lived in their house as mistresses.

The nomads had a very beautiful young girl with them. Her name was Chhabeeli. Glistening tanned complexion, sharp features, sculpted figure, large green eyes, light brown long hair, a sweet voice like the tinkling of silver bells, a laughter like a gently cascading water fall, beautiful as in fairy tales. The chief of the nomads, who controlled all the finances knew her worth, and had firmly refused the offer of several rich farmers to take her as a mistress for a fee. He waited.

Samarjeet was middle aged by then and his only son had gone to England for education. May be, that he was passing through a depression at the thought that the English may leave India. May be, that he was bored with the cultivated mannerisms of the courtesans and dancing girls, who came to entertain him and his numerous guests. Or, perhaps the ancient feudal blood in his veins had defeated the norms of controlled behaviour- that he had adopted during his stay in the West, and he was ready to take a plunge into the lake of pleasures, which had been the playground of his ancestors, for generations. So, when his servants brought the news of the girl, dancing in gatherings of villagers, her skirt swirling well above her knees, a dhapali (a hand held flat drum) in her hand, singing joyfully, her eyes twinkling with the joy of being alive, his curiosity was aroused.

Before long the leader of the nomads got a call from the villa, to perform. All the women and the young girls of the nomads put on their best, and when it was getting dark they assembled in the large courtyard of the villa. The servants of the Thakur made seating arrangements, chairs for rich farmers and upper caste villagers, durries for the other villagers, and a separate arrangement for the women.

After some pleasantries were exchanged, betel etc. were passed around. Soon the performances started and picked up. Chhabeeli's dance immediately caught the attention of the Thakur. The gathering took a note of it and held its breath. Oblivious to all the silent commotion that her beauty, her charm, her youth, her swirling skirts, and sweat covered face glistening in the light thrown by Petromax lamps and her sensuous lilting voice was causing, Chhabeeli danced, while the men accompanying her played various musical instruments.

Soon she was asked by the Thakur to perform alone and he showered her with money, which was collected by the leader. The leader stepped forward and told the Thakur in measured court-language that he had saved her for a true 'connoisseur'. The hint was obvious. By that time, the eyes of the Thakur were red with wine and desire and his clerk offered a sum of twenty thousand rupees to the leader to "take Chhabeeli for life". The leader had received offers of larger sums from the dancing houses in the city, and he could have kept her "unattached" and continue to cash in on her charms, but he knew that he could easily lose his life if he refused. He requested the Thakur to be generous and reconsider his offer since the girl was to be lost to the clan. Thakur in a fit of desire raised the sum to fifty thousand rupees and told that the nomads were never to meet her again, and leave immediately. The leader collected the sum, left Chhabeeli standing there and departed with his followers. No one paid any attention to the young nomad of the clan, who walked away slowly, completely forlorn, a flute in his hand, a flute he had played with élan, during the performance.

Resistance to Thakur's act came from an unexpected quarter. His wife announced that she would leave the villa, if Chhabeeli as much as even stepped into it. Thakur was taken aback. He hardly ever met his wife. She was rumoured to be unattractive and obstinate. But she had given him a son. She was also the daughter of a very rich landlord and the Thakur knew that he could not afford to make his father-in-law angry. Chhabeeli was kept in the outhouse, where he went every evening. He got some women to tutor her and to prepare her to be a host to his friends. She was forbidden to dance but she was tutored by Ustads to sing gazals and as well as khayaals. Chhabeeli turned out to be a good student and learnt quickly.

The Thakur also started constructing a hunting lodge in the forest. There were no large game in the forest and the lodge was to be his pleasure house. It was ready soon. It had several large rooms and a garden. It was surrounded by high boundary walls and protected by an imposing iron gate. The villagers, summoned to work on the construction never stepped into the lodge once it was ready. They only saw luxury goods being taken into the forest on camels and mules from time to time.

Thakur was madly in love with the girl and he spent most of his time in the hunting lodge. Once in a while, the two came out on horses to explore the forest or to have a picnic near one of the many lakes, where servants put up a large fare for their pleasure. Villages for tens of miles around, talked of the love affair between an England educated Thakur and a nomad girl and waited for further developments.

Then the Thakur had to accompany a large hunting party to the border of Nepal. He was to be away for almost three months. As the hunting was only a ruse by the rich landlords of the area and the small kings and nawabs, to discuss the strategy for dealing with the situation arising out of the likely departure of British, Chhabeeli was left behind. He ordered his clerk to look after her and he in turn put his son in charge of her welfare.

The nomads had not come to the village for almost five years. And then one night the villagers were awakened by tunes of a very soulful song played on a flute. It was a heart rending song. Next morning they found a young nomad named Baanke, camping alone near the ravines, with his dark ferocious dog. He did not talk much, fished in the river, or trapped birds to eat and sang and played the flute throughout the night. And then he was gone, along with his dog. People got busy with their routine, till they heard very faint sounds of his flute coming from the forest, from the direction of the hunting lodge.

This continued for about a month when the Thakur returned. He first went to his villa and later as the evening approached he went to the lodge. Chhabeeli looked very pleased to see him and laid out the best wines and meats to welcome him and as the night progressed she sang gazals for him.

Thakur awoke during the night, hearing a soulful tune played on a flute accompanied by a song and Chhabeeli missing from his side. He got up and looked out. He found the guard missing from the gate and two shadows in embrace. He came back and lay still as if asleep. A little later Chhabeeli returned and lay by his side.

Thakur went back to his villa in the morning. He did that often, when work demanded his personal intervention. On such days, when he returned, he brought gifts of sweets, wines, dresses, etc. for Chhabeeli. He returned in the evening and asked for some wine to be served. And then, as if he remembered something, he ordered the servants to bring the food packet he had left with his clerk, who was waiting outside.

He asked Chhabeeli to serve the kabobs that he had brought. As Chhabeeli ate the kabobs, which Thakur took on his plate but avoided eating, he watched her face closely. He watched her chew on the liver. Then he asked her, if she noticed any difference. When she said that she did not, he asked her if she could hear a flute as she ate. Chhabeeli's face turned ashen and she fainted.

Thakur left her there and went back to his villa. The next day he left for Allahabad and never returned to the village. He died of a devastated liver, some years later. No one ever heard the flute again.

Chhabeeli stayed on in the lodge or rather she was not allowed to leave it by Thakur's wife, who continued to provide her with food and clothing but not much else. All the luxury goods in the hunting lodge were removed and auctioned. No one was allowed to meet Chhabeeli.

Then, one day, Thakur's wife received a request to provide Chhabeeli a talking myna. She took a pity on Chhabeeli and sent her several mynas from Himalayas, which are famous for their skill in imitating a human voice.

India became independent a little before Thakur's death, and his son was called back to look after his vast estate's affairs. The absence of his father from the scene for several years had taken its toll. However the son was very worldly-wise and soon put most of the affairs of estate in order, with the help of the trusted clerk of his father.

Then he went to the hunting lodge with some servants. The iron gate was rusted and groaned loudly as it was opened. Well, it had not been opened since Thakur had last left. The food grains etc. to Chhabeeli used to be given through a small opening in the boundary wall.

At first, he did not find any signs of life in the lodge. But as he entered the main hall, he heard chirping of birds, accompanied by snatches of songs and tunes of a flute. He followed the sound to find Chhabeeli, sitting in the inner courtyard, with a flute in her hand. And then an extraordinary thing happened. Suddenly, some of the mynas burst into a song. As he listened, the birds sang:

'Baanke O Baanke,

I belong to you, and only you.'

And then some other mynas, whistled out the tunes of the flute.

He was overtaken by remorse and touched the feet of Chhabeeli, asking for her forgiveness. He left after telling that the birds were to be released from their cages, while Chabbeeli was to be looked after till she lived. Chhabeeli saw her mynas fly away. She smiled.

She knew that the story of her sale, her captivity, and her love for Baanke would live as long as her disciples, the mynas survived. And her mynas did fly out to villages even far away from Bholaganj, with the song and the tune on their beaks. Some of them occasionally flew back to the hunting lodge and sang to Chhabeeli.

One day, one of them came to the villa of the Thakur. His wife heard the song. She looked at the framed photograph of her husband, and whispered, 'Did you hear that Thakur?'

The bird flew away.

4

A Handful of Grain

When we moved to an apartment in the suburbs of Kolkata, we felt very lonely. We did not know any one. We had no idea, which vegetable vendor would advise us against buying a particular item if it was not good. We did not know which washerman would be regular and which newspaperman would give us the papers, regularly and in time. I would stand in the balcony and look out in search of a smile and return, quite frustrated. The rooms looked different. The position of the bed did not seem right. The sunlight entered the rooms at an odd angle. The neighbours had noisy cars. The dogs barked all night. The traffic on the neighbouring road roared throughout the night. We could not sleep well and were permanently irritated.

And then, one day a sparrow entered our drawing room, flying from chair to chair, and from table to the ceiling fans and from carpet to the sofa. I watched in fascination as its tail went up and down and it chirped in several different ways. Soon it was joined by its mate. They flew around the room for some more time and then flew away. Our daughter came out and sneered that they would leave bird droppings around and we should not encourage them. But for the first time in several days, I found myself slightly relaxed. I returned from my office in the evening and found a small feather on my study table and some bird droppings near the window. I removed the droppings from the window and touched the feather gently, rejoicing in its silken touch. I slept well for the first time after moving to the new apartment.

Next day I opened all the windows and the door to the balcony and sat down to read the newspaper. In a few minutes, the sparrows returned, chirping and flying from chair to the ceiling fan to the sofa. I did not want them to fly away. They had filled the room with warmth and a soothing music which I had been looking for days. I went to the kitchen, took out a handful of uncooked rice and spread it in the balcony. The sparrows went to the balcony and picked a few grains. And then they sat on the railings and chirped differently. Soon there were several sparrows, chirping happily, flying around, flying in, flying out, flying from chairs to the sofa to the paintings on the wall to the light fixtures. I sat there completely relaxed, watching them, happy.

Soon it became my routine. I would get up in the morning, and put out a handful of rice in the balcony. The sparrows would come and finish it in half an hour or so, picking every grain. Then one day, two shaligs joined them, tasted the rice, approved of it and they also started coming every day. One or two crows came occasionally, but were easily lured away by our neighbours throwing out pieces of bread or leftovers, from their kitchens.

I was happy again and relaxed. I slowly started to get to know the vegetable vendors, developed a smiling acquaintance with the owner of the grocery shop and found myself whistling again as I went down the stairs. The birds started assembling on the railings of the balcony every day. They would start an orchestra, if we were late in giving them the rice. I told my daughter that they reminded me of a folk song; "Father, I was a sparrow in your courtyard, why did you marry me off to a place so far away?" She laughed and remarked, "Aha, so now they are your daughters, eh?" But she never failed to inform me that the birds were being fed, whenever I was away from the city and she never failed to mention that they always finished the rice, down to the last grain.

By this time I had become quite relaxed, I had started eating well again and it showed. In any case I have been overweight for years. Considering my advancing years, our doctor advised me to do something about it and called me for a checkup. He insisted that I lose weight and eat as much salad as possible.

Now, I have never liked salads in my life. Salad for me, at the most means slices of tomato and onion and some chilli with a sprinkling of salt, pepper, lemon, and coriander leaves. I have never liked lettuce. It was then that my wife thought of getting sprouted gram and moong for me. She chalked out a schedule of keeping them soaked in water for one night and then draining the water and hanging them overnight, tied to a cloth. She proudly served a plateful of sprouted moongs with a slice of lemon and some salt. She took a plate herself and started eating it with relish.

I took a spoonful of sprouts and before I knew I felt a severe nausea and ran to the bath room to throw up. She took a spoonful of the sprouts from my plate and found nothing wrong. She was amused at my discomfort and told that I would get used to it.

However, same thing happened the next day, and the day after. I was perplexed myself, as she has the most delicate stomach in the family and even the slightest problem with food gives her a dysentery or nausea or stomachache. We pride ourselves as a rational family. And we felt that it was a completely irrational reaction to a simple change of diet.

I talked to our doctor and he laughed. He remarked that I was looking for an excuse to eat rich foods. But then on a more serious note he asked me to try to remember if the sprouts reminded me of some unusual incident. I raked my memory to no avail. And then I called my mother. She listened to me quietly. She narrated the following and told that I was about four years old when it happened. The incident surely lay buried in my subconscious mind, she added.

The old couple lived in a hut at the edge of our village. They were really old and childless. They had no land and were not strong enough to work in the fields. After the harvest was over, they would go from field to field and pick fallen ears of wheat, barley, or paddy. And then they would go from field to field and pick grains of wheat, barley, peas, gram, arahar, moong, or urad. In spite of their abject poverty they were full of cheer. And in spite of their abject poverty, they never begged. When the going was tough they would survive on leaves of wild plants, roots and boiled seeds of mangoes. They never complained and refused to accept any help, which looked like alms.

Perhaps, they would have gone on like this, but then one evening the land lord returning on his horse, noticed them picking ears of wheat which had fallen in the field. He was in a happy frame of mind. The harvest had been good. He alighted from his horse and stood chatting with the old man while the old lady continued to collect the ears of the corn. The horse moved around and found the sack which they had spread to keep the grain. It started feeding on the grain from the sack.

The couple had worked the whole day collecting the grains, ear by ear, grain by grain. The old lady tried to shoo the horse away. The horse was not used to being shooed and continued feeding on the grain. The old lady, in desperation picked up a pebble and threw it at the horse. The horse neighed angrily and stamped its hoofs.

The landlord got furious at the fact that the lady had hit his horse, even though the couple had collected the grain from his fields. He ordered them to leave immediately and shouted that they were not to pick grain from the fields after the harvest. The old couple got up and quietly walked back to their hut. The news spread all over the village. But no one could do anything about it. Most of the land in the village belonged to the landlord and most of the people in the village worked on his fields. No one dared to help them in any way.

During those days, grains of wheat or barley used to be separated from the stalks with the help of oxen. The stacks of dry stalks of wheat or barley used to be spread out in a circle and then oxen would be made to walk on it.

The dry stalks would, after some time, be converted into chaff which would then be poured from a height of a few feet against wind to separate the grain from it. As the oxen went round and round on the stalks, they continued to feed on the stalks and chaff along with the grain. As the entire produce was a result of the hard work of the oxen, it was considered a sin to stop them from feeding on the grain.

The old couple had not eaten for two days. There was simply nothing for them to eat. They walked slowly, leaning heavily on their stick and came to rest at the place where the dung of the oxen of the landlord used to be heaped. They sat there and started picking undigested grains from the dung heap. Several of these had already sprouted. They came back and washed the grain, and put it in an earthen pot to boil.

Seeing the smoke coming from their hut, the landlord was surprised. He had wanted them to beg for food. He had wanted them to admit that they lived on his mercy. The old couple had not begged. The old couple had not asked for forgiveness for shooing away the horse of the landlord. And they were cooking food! The landlord, my father, asked a servant to go and find out what they were cooking. How could they cook anything? Had they stolen some grain? Had someone from the village defied him and helped?

I had insisted on going with him.

That was my first visit to their hut or any hut for that matter. I had been surprised to find it so bare. In one corner on a sack lay some grain, partly sprouted, cow dung still sticking to them, spread out to dry. I had peeped into the pot and seen the same grain being boiled. My mother told that I had started throwing up then and there and was very ill for several months. My deliriums had helped her piece together these happening.

And now as I see the sparrows picking rice, grain by grain, in my balcony, I think about an old couple, who lived by picking grain from our fields after harvest, and who knew the meaning of hunger, which I was not destined to know, and whose memory had been obliterated from my mind. I wanted to ask my mother, whether the old couple had really forgiven my father, when he had asked them to pick grain from the fields, again. I realized that I did not have the courage to face the answer.

I still can't eat sprouted grains, as now I am blinded by tears when I see them.

5

Flowers of Mahua

Being a villager, I pity the city-bred people. I pity their ability to say 'yes' when they mean 'no'. I pity their ability to produce a smile which hides their true intentions. I pity their arrogance and their belief that the whole universe should work for their pleasure. I pity their unabashed selfishness. And I pity their disdain of villagers, which of course is a ruse and a strategy to get the village produce very cheaply.

I pity them as they have no roots to lose. I pity them for they will never know the pains of a refugee and a migrant worker. I pity them for they will not know that when the morning approaches and the Venus rises in the east, the horizon turns orange, birds sing their morning song, and peacocks fill the universe with their call. And I pity them for they will not know that when the evening descends, birds return home and stars appear one by one and slowly fill the sky. I pity them for they will not see the Sapta Rishis start their journey around the pole star and the moon spread a shiny sheet of gentle light over the swaying fields of grain. I pity them for they will never hear the call of jackals, the night watchmen of the jungle, calling every hour; first one, then two, and then their whole party. I pity them for they will never see the millions of stars 'flowing' in the Ganges of The Sky. And I pity them for they will never see my grandmother who died a long time ago, still go to pick flowers of mahua trees, which were sold, felled, and converted to planks and charcoal soon after her death.

Our orchard had several mahua trees, many growing to their full height of several tens of feet. They had large, thick, and sturdy branches, spreading over a huge area around them. Their foliage was so thick that if you took a shelter under them in a mild rain, you would not get wet. And there was always a cool shade and a breeze under them, even when the skies rained fire and brimstone in summer. And they were so gentle that when you broke or even folded the leaves or the branch-lets, the milk running in their veins covered your hands. The older branches had holes which housed parrots, woodpeckers, and squirrels. A group of monkeys often came and camped on them for days. Crows and mynahs and babblers and doves made their nests on them. Several hoopoes and woodpeckers constantly moved up and down their trunks and branches, pecking at the insects thriving under the bark. All kinds of ants, large and small, raced along the trunks, carrying food for storage. A kind of leaf stitching ants lived on the trees who stitched together several leaves, wrapping them in a silken web and making a fairly large sized nest.

As winter approached, the 'mushahars' came and asked my grandfather for a permission to take leaves from the mahua trees. They also took leaves from the neem tree and used the rachis of the neem leaves to pin the leaves of mahua together and make 'donas' (small cups) and 'pattals' (plates) to be used during village feasts. With the peaking of the winter, the mahua trees shed their leaves which dried quickly and filled the orchard with a heady smell of freshness.

We collected these brown-red-rust leaves to be spread under our cows to make a warm and cozy bed for them and to convert their droppings to manure for our fields. And we collected the leaves to have a fire in the evening. We sat around it listening to stories and roasting sweet potatoes, green grams and peas and ears of unripe wheat and barley. We collected the ash and sprinkled it on the leaves of plants of brinjal and creepers of pumpkin growing in our vegetable patch to protect them from caterpillars. We made a heap of the leaves along with wood and cow dung cakes to make the huge bonfire of Holi; various groups of the village having a competition about the height of the flames. The leaves were especially useful when we sprained our legs or some muscle, as our grandmother would tie a leaf of mahua with a paste of turmeric, heated with mustard oil. The pain would soon be gone.

By mid-April the trees would be bare of leaves and slowly they would be covered with bunches of flowers, in various stages of bloom. Our grandmother would get the area under them cleaned and polished with cow dung and clay. The flowers would start dropping by midnight making a soft sound as they landed, splattering some of their sweet juice around them. Slowly their smell would start spreading across the village and beyond it. Neelgais and even jackals living in the forest near our village traveled almost a mile to eat them in a hurried manner. Our grandmother told of a time when a herd of wild elephants had come to feast on them and not being satisfied with picking them one by one, had pulled down several branches of the trees. There was a time when the forest near our village had deer and wild boars and they also came and claimed their share.

The cream-coloured flowers looked like large pearls of the size of eggs of pigeons. They had a thick-fleshy body, with a narrow hole running through them. Tiny rust-coloured stamens stuck to the inner walls of the hole and its mouth on one side was covered with tiny green leafy petals. You could remove the petals, blow out the stamens, and eat the flowers which had a heavenly taste. No wonder that mahua was called the grape of the poor.

The wives and daughters of our workers would arrive in the morning with baskets to pick the flowers. First, our grandmother would ask them to sweep a pathway through the carpet of flowers covering the whole ground so that no one walked on them. Crows and sparrows and mynahs and ants would already be feasting on them, while flocks of parrots would be covering the tree with a vibrant green, screeching and feeding on flowers which had not yet blossomed fully. The women would pick the flowers and take home one third or one fourth of them as wages. The rest would be spread to dry in the sun.

All the trees had names and their flowers had distinct tastes and flavours. Of all our trees, two were very special. One was called Gularahawa (fig-like) and the other was called Cowriyaa (cowry-like). As the name suggests, the flowers of Gularahawa were large and fleshy. They were also extremely sweet. My mother would take the flowers of Gularahawa and squeeze them, collecting the juice in a large wooden pot. The pulp would be mixed with fodder to be given to cows. The watery- milk coloured juice would soon fill the house with a strong musky aroma. She would occasionally add a little flour and then pour the juice in a wok to boil. Soon the juice would turn to a thick paste. We ate it with our fingers or with chapattis for breakfast or lunch.

The pudding of flowers from Gularahawa was well known for its flavour, smell and taste and people from even neighbouring villages came to exchange their mahua flowers with its flowers, giving up to one and half times more flowers in return.

The flowers of Cowriyaa were not that soft and were somewhat smaller and almost white. But the tree compensated for their size by producing them in plenty. They also had a splendid bitter taste and were famed for curing men and animals of indigestion and cold, when dried. The flowers of Cowriyaa were dried separately and stored separately.

In about two months of flowering, fifty, sixty, or even a hundred kilograms of dried flowers would be collected from every tree, put into gunny bags, and stored in the room full of chaff, which would have come from the harvest of wheat, earlier. By early June the trees would sprout new leaves, in gorgeous colours of rust and crimson, turning rapidly to a polished shiny light green and then dark green. Then the fruits would appear. When fully grown, they would be almost as large as a lemon and would have one, two, or three, or sometimes even four glassy brown rust coloured shining seeds. The pulp of the fruit, when raw, was cooked by our mother using the smallest amount of mustard oil and spices, as a vegetable. As the fruits ripened, they fell to the ground. The birds loved the ripening pulp.

The women collected the fruits; removing the pulp, by now soft and yellow to be fed to cows. The seeds were split and dried and taken by the teli- the oil man, who crushed it on his ox-driven oil mill and gave us the oil and cakes. The cakes were stored and later mixed with the fodder for the animals. The oil looked like molten butter and we used it in our lamps. The village trader bought it from us for the soap and candle factories in the city. Our grandmother sold it to our workers who even used it for cooking. The oil of Cowriyaa was especially in demand as it was also known to cure rheumatism.

If someone needed timber for making a house, he would approach us almost a year and half in advance, select a branch, and cut it after offering prayer to all the spirits of the tree. He would remove the bark and put the wood in the village pond for seasoning for almost a year, before taking it out to dry in shade for months and using for the house under construction.

We, as well as the workers on our fields, ate the dried mahua flowers in several ways. The flowers were just roasted on a hot plate and eaten with parched grain. They were also boiled with pea or wheat or gram and eaten, or they were eaten just raw. When we employed the workers to clean the well or to make a rope or to thatch the roof for the cow shed, we would give them the dried mahua flowers as wages.

Well this would have gone on till eternity, as it has been going on since eternity. But then, Rajaram, the son of one of the workers on our field went to Calcutta. He returned to the village during one of his holidays, complete with a shining white dhoti, umbrella, pump shoes, and oiled hair. All the young men in the village assembled in his house in the evening and he treated them to liquor.

Now, many workers from our village smoked marijuana once in a while, as it was customary for the rich farmers to treat them to it especially after a good harvest or during Holi. But none ever consumed liquor, though it was rumoured that some of the big farmers drank occasionally, especially during weddings and after a good harvest. In any case, Rajaram soon ran out of the liquor he had brought and decided to make some of his own. He took the dried mahua collected by his mother from our orchard, soaked it in water and distilled it after a few days. The effect of the liquor could be heard every evening from his house. The young men assembled more and more often at his house. He discovered that the flowers from the Cowriyaa gave the best liquor. However, soon enough, he ran out of the mahua flowers- including those with all his friends. We could hear quarrels and shouting by their women complaining about w h a t they were going to eat during the lean months.

So it happened that one day Rajaram came to our house and asked to buy dried flowers of Cowriyaa. He knew that we stored them separately because of their medicinal properties, especially against their effectiveness against cold. My grandfather had often expressed his disgust at the distillery operating in Rajaram's house and was surprised that he had been unable to find support among the workers of the village to stop it.

Hearing that Rajaram had come to buy flowers of mahua, my mother, who observed strict 'purdah' (veil), went to main door. She pulled her sari over her face and rattled the iron chain of the door to attract the attention of the menfolk outside the house. When our grandfather turned, she told very firmly that no flowers should be sold to Rajaram. She also hinted that she had seen our uncle going out late in the night and returning quite tipsy, but had kept silent to avoid a family feud.

Rajaram left then but came several times again, only to hear a firm 'no' from my grandfather. Then he stopped coming. One day, my mother went to the room where mahua flowers were stocked to get some flowers from Cowriyaa to boil as several of us had caught cold. She was surprised to find that several sacks of flowers were missing. She realized that our uncle was taking them away. The discovery led to an angry quarrel between my uncle and grandfather. Our uncle left the house to go to Calcutta along with Rajaram.

He returned some years later, with Rajaram. Both our grandparents had passed away by then. Our uncle asked for a partitioning of our ancestral properties. The orchard was partitioned by a throw of marked sticks of neem. As fate would have it, three throws in a row gave him a control of the portion having all the mahua trees while we got the portion having mango and neem trees. That year, when mahua flowers bloomed he and Rajaram, who had come on a long holiday, started a distillery to make liquor in bulk. The liquors from the flowers from Cowriyaa and the Gularahawa were specially prized and sold separately.

My uncle was often found quite drunk and abusive, even during the day. Soon it was time for the mahua to stop giving flowers and to start giving fruits. My uncle was by then quite addicted to his large intake of drinks, and when he did not get any in the house, he went to the city to buy some. He was surprised to know the high cost of the liquor in the city, which he and Rajaram used to sell so cheaply. He tried to buy some on a credit, but no one knew him there. While he sat fretting and cursing, the saw mill owner of the city met him and offered to buy his trees. We came to know that he gave cash to my uncle, who purchased some liquor and sat down to party. He was surprised to find so many people who were friendly to him, where none had talked to him a little earlier.

The saw mill owner came with his men, the same afternoon. They soon got to work and by evening the trees were felled one by one. They made a deafening sound as they fell, which was pierced by the sound of its breaking branches and the painful screams of birds and squirrels who ran all over the place. We saw so many destroyed nests and broken eggs. And we saw baby birds and baby squirrels falling to their death. A silence descended on our house as my mother sat crying in front of the photographs of our grandparents.

Our uncle returned after three days. As he stood where the mahua trees had stood and looked around, he saw a desolate piece of land. He went inside his house and closed his doors. A few days later, he went back to Calcutta and never returned.

Time passed and it was season for the mahuas to flower again. One day, my mother woke up very early in the morning. The moon was setting and the Venus was rising in the east. She heard a call of peacocks from somewhere far away. She opened the window. As she looked out, she saw our grandmother picking mahua flowers from the ground where Gularahawa and Cowriyaa had stood and storing them in separate baskets. A gentle breeze laden with the heady scent of flowers of mahua started blowing. Before she could wake us up, the breeze was gone and so was our grandmother.

Years have passed since that day. Nothing, not even a blade of grass, grows there. Yet people say that every year when it is time to pick flowers of mahua, a breeze laden with the heady scent of mahua flowers blows there and our grandmother can be seen picking and storing the flowers in two separate baskets.

6

Jatak Tales

Neeraj sat in the balcony. It was still rather early in the morning. The sun was up but it was still cold. The maid had put his easy chair, the newspaper, his book, his glasses, and a jug of water there. She had also put a light woolen shawl there. And she had put some raw rice in a bowl. It was as before. It was as on every day, since the last many years. It was so since Uma had left him to be with her many gods.

His son and daughter lived in America. They called every week, enquired about his health and the weather. They reminded him to get regular medical checkups done. They asked him to keep getting his pass-book updated to make sure that the money they sent him had reached. They requested him to call them whenever he felt like or whenever he was not well- even if it was just a simple cold or indigestion. They asked him to go to USA, but he always refused. He did not want to be a burden to them. He was quite all right, he told them. The maid was very loving and regular.

He slowly walked to the balcony. The sparrows, they had befriended over years, had already started assembling there. He still remembered that day, some years ago, when a sparrow with a broken leg and a damaged wing had landed in their balcony. Uma had picked up the frightened bird and tended it back to health. She had tried to feed it a variety of foods and then as if by mutual agreement, the two had settled on raw rice. The sparrow had followed her around the house; almost like her son who was always following her-even when his sister teased him. Then one day it had flown away, only to return in the morning. Uma had gone running to the balcony to see it. And, she had brought a handful of rice. As she had spread her palm, the sparrow had eaten some rice eagerly and had flown away. Uma had waited for the sparrow and after getting tired, had left a handful of rice there. A little later the balcony was full of sparrows and it was with a great difficulty that she had recognized 'her' sparrow. Ever since then, it had become their favourite game. Neeraj would sit in the easy-chair and put out a handful of rice on the wooden plate that Uma had fixed to the railing, replenishing it every now and then. Uma sat too, chopping vegetables, cleaning rice, knitting sweaters, reading, or just watching the birds. The water bowl had come much later; after they had read that normally more than eighty percent of birds died of thirst. Even when Uma was in hospital, she had sent him back every day to put plenty of rice in the plate and to fill the water bowl.

He took out a handful of raw rice and put it in the wooden plate. He saw that the water bowl was a little less than full. He slowly walked to the kitchen and got a glass of water to fill the bowl. Then he sat down to watch the birds. They came in groups of twos and threes and fours. They jumped around, chirped and ate the rice. They flew away and came back again after some time. One group of the birds flew away and another came. He was reminded of waves at a sea beach as he saw them. It had always given him peace and tranquility, even when their son had left for USA, even when their daughter had left to join him, and even when Uma had left him.

Neeraj noted that there were some smaller birds who flew around clumsily and whose beaks were still translucent. He knew they were babies, still learning to fly and eat. Their parents would take a grain of rice and put it in their beaks, before eating themselves.

He remembered how Uma always fed the children before she ate. He remembered how their son ran around the house as Uma ran after him with food in a bowl, cajoling; 'this one for Papa', 'this one for Mummy', 'this one for Didi', 'this one for Grandma', 'this one for Grandpa', 'this one for the sparrow', 'this one for the cow', and wiping his face with her 'aanchal' after every morsel. Their son would run, try to hide, fall, laugh or cry and get up and run again, giggling and dancing.

Years later, when his daughter had come with her child, he had noted with a smile that his grandchild had run around the flat and his daughter had chased him, cajoling and feeding him morsel by morsel; 'this one for Papa', 'this one for Mummy', 'this one for Grandpa', 'this one Grandma'. Uma had smiled too and had recalled how she had to invent a new ruse every day to feed their daughter. He would go around with his grandchild, showing him the garden, the cars, the market, the cows, as he had shown them to his children. He remembered how his children were always eager to go out with him to marvel at the world. He remembered how Uma had used that period to quickly prepare meals and complete other jobs.

The birds had finished the last grain of rice and were now jumping around and chirping noisily. He took another handful of rice and put it in the wooden plate. He sat down, wrapped the shawl around him, picked up the book and read about earlier births of Lord Buddha.

'Once upon a time a group of wood-cutters came across an elephant in a forest. The elephant was injured and in severe pain. They saw that a thick and sharp splinter of wood had pierced its foot and it was limping. They took courage, went near the elephant and pulled out the splinter. One of them used his turban to tie the bleeding leg after applying a paste of medicinal leaves. A few days later the elephant approached them and looking at the tree which they were cutting, pulled it down. When they had trimmed it, he lifted it using his trunk and carried it to the edge of the forest. It started coming every day to help the wood-cutters.

Many years passed. The elephant grew old. Then one day he brought his son, a most majestic white elephant. The baby elephant began to help the wood-cutters too with his limited strength and played with their children, taking them across the river and bathing them. ..'.

Neeraj looked at the birds; they had come with their babies to give him company. Like his daughter; who had come with her son to give him company. Like his son; who had telephoned that he was reaching in a week along with his daughter and wife. He smiled and felt a drowsiness coming over him. The book fell from his hands.

They found him sitting with a smile on his face. His neighbour picked up the book. It was a volume of Jatak Tales. The inscription was signed on the same day. It read, 'With love and best wishes to Sunny-from Grandpa.'

7

A Leaf of Tulsi

It was rather warm and I decided to sit in the lawn of the motel in Lafayette, where I was staying. I had gone to the Purdue University for a conference. Most of the other delegates were staying near the university. I sat alone and looked at the sun as it slowly sank beneath the horizon, leaving a glowing colourful cloud in its wake. I had not noticed Vivek. He had walked silently and stood behind me looking at those very clouds. I turned back when he gently coughed. I had seen him during the conference but there had been far too many people surrounding him. I had noted that he was the only other Indian in the meeting. I asked him to have a seat. He sat down and introduced himself. We started talking.

Of course I had heard of him. In fact, the newspapers of the day had carried a long interview with him along with his photograph. He was from University of California at Berkeley and his work in the field of astronomy was very well recognized. He was telling me about his work, when he stopped in mid-sentence and got up.

I followed his gaze to the small house towards the back of the motel. An elderly woman in a sari, her head covered, a small lamp in her hands, was going around a potted plant in front of the house. It did not take us long to realize that she was performing Tulsi-puja, as millions of women in India have done for hundreds of years. We waited for her to finish and slowly approached her. She had noticed us and waited for us. She offered us crystal sugar and leaves of Tulsi. She blessed us profusely as we reverentially touched her feet. No introductions were necessary and we walked back silently to our seats. Her simple gestures triggered varied emotions in our minds. This is the story of Vivek, or rather his mother, in his own words.

My mother belonged to a generation where women of good families never crossed the threshold of the house into which they were married. Thus confined, she created a world of her own-which centred on her family: my father, me, gods and goddesses, various festivals, fasts, and rituals. She ventured out only very occasionally, that also only after my father's death, when it became essential for her. I wonder how she lived all those years, confined within the four walls of the house. She never complained. She even avoided talking directly to my father. When she wanted to tell him something, she would ask me to 'tell father'.

When she needed to call us inside the house, she stood behind the door and gently rattled the chain holding the doors. If she knew that we were close by, she would just shake her hands, producing a gentle tinkle of her glass bangles. Only women, small children, and the family priest could come inside the house.

Every evening, as our cows returned from the grazing fields and the sun dipped below the horizon, she lit a lamp of pure ghee near the Tulsi (basil) plant in our courtyard and walked around it three times with folded hands. Every morning, after a bath, she offered water from a shiny brass pot to the Tulsi plant. She went around it three times keeping the plant on her right, saying prayers and offering a bit of water as she completed the round. The regularity and the constancy of this act gave me a feeling of strong comfort and bliss. This is one of my fondest memories and somehow that is how I remember my mother.

Whenever I had a fever, she plucked some leaves of Tulsi, and boiled them with black pepper and made me drink that very bitter concoction. I hated the taste, but always felt better afterwards.

She had kept my fever under control with the same concoction, even when I had suffered from malaria. Today I look back and wonder; how she had lived in that remote village armed only with her faith in gods and goddesses and some simple home remedies.

As summer roared and evenings brought a mild breeze, the scorpions with their raised poisonous tails came out in search of food. Being a restless child, running all over the place, I often stepped on them in the dark, only to get a nasty sting. I would scream and my mother would light a lamp and look for the sting, remove the barb and apply a paste of Tulsi leaves.

Diarrhea was my most common problem during my childhood. She always cured it by giving me some concoction of Tulsi leaves. She cured our coughs by making us chew leaves of Tulsi with ginger and honey. Her whole life revolved around Tulsi and her faith in Tulsi was phenomenal!

She used to hold a Satyanarayan Puja on every full moon

day at our home near the Tulsi plant. The family priest came in the morning and started asking for all the things needed for the Puja. I ran in and out of the house collecting all that he asked for; a tiny branch of mango along with leaves, dry sticks of mango, some sand, various grains, turmeric powder, water, a small plant of banana, cow dung, etc. My mother prepared gently roasted wheat flour, adding sugar or jaggery to it. She prepared the charanamrit-washings off the feet of Lord Shaligram using curd with dry fruits and leaves of Tulsi.

We knew the story by heart, yet we sat around, reverentially, rejoicing at the end of each chapter, when the priest blew his conch shell. I enjoyed these occasions immensely, especially the hawan (the fire sacrifice), while chanting 'swaha' with the priest and offering ghee to the fire, while my mother offered a mixture of barley, rice, sesame, ghee, various incenses and saw-dust of sandalwood. Soon the house was full of mildly scented fumes from the hawan.

The final sounding of conch shell by the priest brought women and children from the neighbourhood in hordes. I used to enjoy this moment, as I could lord over all the kids and offered them smaller or larger quantities of the prasad (offerings) depending on my liking for them.

My mother often sat near the plant, doing simple chores and composing or just singing hymns in praise of various gods and goddesses and of course Ma Tulsi. I found a large notebook of her hymns after her death and some of them were really quite lyrical and moving. It also contained a long lyrical poem describing the humbling of Satyabhama, one of the wives of Lord Krishna, whose entire collection of ornaments could not outweigh Him, while just a leaf of Tulsi outweighed Him.

One day, my father brought her a book on homeopathy along with a small box of medicines. She carefully read the book and started practicing homeopathy. She prescribed medicines in the name of Tulsi Ma. The women of the village came with their children suffering from cold and fever and diarrhoea and worms and boils and dogbites and even injuries. They gathered around her on Tuesdays and Thursdays near the Tulsi plant. She listened to the symptoms and administered medicines, asking them to pray to Tulsi Ma to cure them. If they got better, she made a special offering of jaggery, ghee, and honey during her prayers. I was yet to develop a distrust of homeopathy and it was going to be decades until I was to hear of the placebo effect!

When my father got a job in the city, it was time for us to move. She carefully nursed a seedling of the Tulsi and by the time we were ready to leave, it was a few inches tall. A trusted servant was to look after the house and the fields. My mother repeatedly requested his wife to nurse the original plant, and light a lamp and offer water every day. She had stood near the plant and prayed for a long time with tears in her eyes, before leaving. She never let the pot with the little Tulsi out of her sight in our bullock cart ride of three days, with stops on the way. She prayed and lit a lamp near it when we stopped for a rest in the evening and offered water to it after a bath when we started again in the morning. The Tulsi plant and the Ramayan were her talismans.

We slowly settled in the city. In a few months, the Tulsi plant, installed into a large cemented pot, grew to its full height with many branches. My mother became popular in the neighbourhood, with her knowledge of home-remedies, many of which used leaves of Tulsi from our house. Yes, her faith in Tulsi was supreme!

I also saw the first and the only fight between my father and mother around this time. As my mother was very religious, nonvegetarian meals were never prepared in our house. My father had developed a taste for meat in company of his friends and one day he brought some cooked meat to the house. Just as he was looking for a place to keep it, someone called him at the door. He left the pot with the meat on the platform around the Tulsi plant and went to see the person.

My mother screamed, shouted, wept, and prayed in turn, apologizing to Ma Tulsi on behalf of her ignorant husband. By morning, my father was quite subdued and my mother was shivering with fever. She whispered to me to tell father that she had to go to the village to bring back Ma Tulsi, who had surely deserted us because of his wanton act. He quietly arranged for us to travel to the village. During those three days, my mother lived on water. As she alighted from the bullock cart, she ran inside and wept profusely near the plant nursed daily by our servant's wife. We journeyed back with a new seedling, which was 'installed' afresh in our house. My father gave up meat altogether. Our life returned to our daily routine.

To her regular gathering of women, she started reciting from the Ramayan and often asked me to recite and read out the meaning, when she was tired. Occasionally, she organized continuous recitation of the Ramayan from the beginning to the end. She took turns with me and some literate women of the neighbourhood, to recite it. She distributed simple offerings of

Tulsi leaves and crystal sugar or jaggery, when it was over. Though tired, her face would glow with reverence and bliss on such occasions. I went to all my tests, examinations, and competitions with a leaf of Tulsi in my mouth and a mark of turmeric and raw rice in the middle of my forehead. I had to offer the result cards and the trophies to Ma Tulsi before showing them to my father. Several years later, I left for California with a leaf of Tulsi in my mouth, a mark of turmeric and raw rice on my forehead, blessings of my parents on my head and tears of my mother behind me.

She had wanted just one promise from me. She wanted me to return to India to offer her Tulsi leaves with the holy water from the Ganges, when her time came. When I decided to settle down in California, she reminded me of the promise I had made to her, especially as my father had passed away. I requested her to accompany me to our new house. She refused at first, when I told her that she could not carry a Tulsi plant with her. Yet, the lure of being with her grandchild broke her resolve.

She was very happy to see that we had a big lawn with a hedge of roses around it. I often saw her working in the rose bed and watering the lawns and other plants. She had brought seeds of Tulsi with her. She planted them and nursed them to several large plants. She treated our guests to the tea she made with leaves of Tulsi, ginger, and honey. I would often see her sitting with Mary; my wife, playing with the baby or patting him to sleep and chatting amicably, even though she spoke no English and Mary spoke only a smattering of Hindi. On these occasions, her face glowed with warmth, affection, and fulfillment. Soon enough, my mother happily incorporated Christ into her pantheon. She had learnt from Mary, who was Greek, that, Tulsi had grown over the tomb of Christ. She started offering leaves of Tulsi and a lamp at the little altar Mary had in the house. I found it most amusing but was even more surprised when I found that Mary had continued to offer water to the plant of Tulsi and light a lamp near it every day, after my mother had returned to India.

I tried to get my mother to move to California with us. She firmly refused, telling that she could not leave the house with the memories of my father in it. I succeeded in persuading her to stay in the city, which had better medical facilities.

Occasionally she travelled to our village, which by now had a better connectivity, to inspect our fields and the house which were still in the care of our servant and his wife. I went to India in response to a phone call from our neighbours, that my mother was ill. Even though I knew that she was not keeping good health for some time, her condition was bad beyond my worst fears.

She had lost weight. She moved with the help of a walking stick. A maid helped her with her daily chores. In spite of her recurring cold and fever, she had not given up on her daily rituals of offering prayers to Ma Tulsi twice a day. Her condition improved slightly after she saw me. She asked me to take her to our village, where she had not been able to go for almost two years. I was not prepared, for what I was to see. She had known but had never told me.

The servant had died. His only son was alcoholic and a loafer. He had systematically pillaged our house, the surrounding mango orchard, and the fields. He had cut and sold several trees and taken a loan against the fields. However, that was not all! First, he had sold the doors, the windows, the cots, and the vessels of the house. Then he had sold the fired clay tiles, which had covered the roof of our house. Finally, he had sold all the seasoned wood, which had supported the roof on the clay walls. The two intervening monsoons had reduced the walls into a mound of clay.

I looked away while the widow of our servant held on to the feet of my mother and wept, murmuring her helplessness. My mother sat in the car, shedding silent tears. I slowly walked to the spot where our house had once stood. Several small trees of acacia, neem, and peepal were growing where I had played as a child and where my mother had sat and dispensed medicines to the simple women of the village. So many memories came flooding back to me and a lump started rising in my throat. I was almost turning away when I noticed something familiar.

I saw the large cemented pot, which used to hold the Tulsi plant of my mother, lying on its side, almost completely buried under a heap of soil and grass. I slowly walked to it and called out to my mother. Near one of the small trees of peepal, surrounded by grass, several inches tall, we saw several plants of Tulsi, growing lustily and swaying in the breeze. My mother wiped her tears and asked the widowed wife of our servant to get her clothes from the car and fresh water from the well. She prayed for a long time and lit a lamp near the Tulsi plants. We cleaned the pot, filled it with fresh soil, and planted several sturdy plants of Tulsi in it.

My mother rested for a while and then asked me to call the

doctor of the village dispensary. She donated the land and the orchard surrounding the house to the dispensary and asked me to sell the fields and give the proceeds to the doctor to build a decent hospital. She put only one condition; the potted plants of Tulsi were to be looked after.

When we returned to the city, she complained of being tired. In the morning, she got up, took a bath, offered her prayers to Tulsi, and then sat down with exhaustion. She called me and told me that the time had come for me to fulfill my promise to her. I wept and poured water from the Ganges-kept for this purpose in the house, and a few leaves of Tulsi into her mouth. She closed her eyes and a smile full of bliss covered her face.

I went to see the hospital a year later. They had named it after her-Meera Devi Hospital. I was happy to see that the plants of Tulsi were prospering. The employees, especially the nurses, took good care of the Tulsi plants, and worshipped them on a regular basis. The Tulsi plants she had grown in a corner of our lawn in California survive to this day.

Three years after her death our daughter was born. As I held her, Mary told me that she would call her Vrinda-in the memory our mother and her love for Tulsi. She also told that my mother had confided in her that her maiden name was Vrinda, which is another name for Tulsi. She had adopted the name Meera after her wedding, for the women married into our family had to change their name as well. I called our village and requested them to change the name of the hospital to Vrindavan.

Next morning as we proceeded to Vivek's car to go to the

meeting, the elderly woman, whom we had met the previous evening, called out to us. She put a mark of turmeric powder and rice on our foreheads and gave us each a leaf of Tulsi and crystal sugar. She smiled at Vivek and told him in Gujarati, 'May Tulsi Ma bring you glory'. Vivek's eyes turned moist as he touched her feet. Later, it was my turn to have moist eyes, as Vivek received a standing ovation when he concluded his talk.

I do not know why, but as I joined the clapping, I could not but help think of his mother. I realized that she had lived all her life for others.

Just like the plant of Tulsi, she so revered.

8

Such a Wonderful Journey

It started with my first trip to the University of Jammu. It was still early in the summer but it was very hot and one could come out of the guest house only in the evening. The sun had gone down but there was still a plenty of light. As I walked along with my hosts, I was attracted to a row of trees with rope-like stalks hanging from the branches covered with deep red buds.

At first I thought that they were some flowering creepers. Soon, I realized my mistake. The stalks were growing on the trees. I had a further surprise in store when farther down I saw pumpkin-like large fruits, up to two feet long and several inches wide, with a brown, rough surface. I asked my hosts about the tree. Yes, they said, interesting flowers. But they did not know its name. They had heard though that some people wanted those trees to be cut as the fruits were rather heavy and damaged cars parked under the trees. A pity, I added and hoped that it did not happen.

I asked several people. No one knew its name. They had been planted a long time ago. While returning from a late night dinner, I noted that the flowers were in full bloom. They were pretty and deep red. The stalks covered with these large flowers looked extremely elegant and gave out a faint and pleasant smell. I saw several bats flitting from flower to flower.

I returned to Calcutta and asked the gardens in-charge of our institute about the tree. He did not know of any such tree.

Some years later, my wife and I went to the University of Manipur for a short visit. One morning, while walking around the campus, I spotted the same trees planted in a row. Some fruits had dropped and were lying under the trees. They had cracked open and the seeds were sprouting. It had rained heavily only a few days earlier. I looked around and was very happy to note that I was standing close to the Department of Botany. It was still early and students were slowly coming in. I stopped several of them and asked them about the tree. They had no clue.

This visit to Manipur was very sobering for me. We had earlier gone to see the place where Netaji had hoisted the flag of Free India, the vast and the enchanting Loktak Lake and the beautiful market run by women. We had also purchased some elegantly woven shawls and black rice. We had first seen black rice in Minnesota several years earlier. So much beauty, so much elegance, so many colours, such warmth and heartfelt hospitality, amidst all that violence which lay just below the surface!

We had also seen the place where a large number of Japanese soldiers-sent to a distant land by an arrogant army-had died. What was supposed to have been a victory arch of a colony, had become a memorial surrounded by hedges and several large chunks of granite, arranged to mark a place for prayer. Did their loved ones ever know where they died? Did the loved ones of Indian and English soldiers who also died ever go there? The place had, surprisingly, exuded peace and tranquility.

I had also looked at the road coming from Rangoon and recalled how my grandfather had walked more than one thousand kilometers, from Rangoon to Manipur along with thousands of others, after the Japanese occupation of Burma, along the same road. He used to tell us that many had died on the way and people had walked around the dead bodies to continue on their journey. I wonder, whether a thought had ever occurred to him that his grandson would one day stand on the same road and look in the direction of Rangoon. The money that my grandfather had saved and hidden as gold coins in the folds of his dhoti had been used to build our house in the village, to buy land, and to get my father educated and married.

What if he had perished, like so many others, who had died from disease, snake-bite, malaria, dysentery, or just hunger? In the complete breakdown of the governance during those days of turmoil and war, the news of his death would have never reached our village. Perhaps my grandmother would have waited for years for his return from Rangoon. Perhaps she would have imagined that he had taken a Burmese wife, like so many others were believed to have done. Would my father get the education he had, which got him a good job and a marriage into a good family? Would I have been born where I was?

It was the last day of our stay in Imphal and we went for a walk in the university campus again, admiring the batches of students jogging, exercising, and playing games. The aimless walk again brought us near the trees with flowers and large fruits hanging on stalks. I looked around and saw a person hanging a banner for a management conference. I decided to ask him. He did not know the name, but yes, he had also seen them at

University of Jammu, where he had had his education!

While leaving Imphal, I casually mentioned this to my host. "Oh, that pumpkin tree!", he exclaimed. It was quite common in Manipur, he told. The locals used its fruit to treat diabetes. He added with a smile that women rubbed its pulp to firm up their breasts! We parted with a laugh.

Coming back to Calcutta, I searched for pumpkin tree, brown pumpkin, and even expanded it to look for, cucumber tree, brown cucumbers, and even brown bottle-gourd on the web. No luck. One day seeing me search for trees with large fruits on the web, my wife remarked, "But those fruits looked so much like large sausages"!

Even though I was skeptical, I looked for sausage tree. Whoa! Immediately it popped out-Sausage Tree-Kigelia Africana, complete with photographs and descriptions of the tree, its dark green leaves, its deep red flowers hanging on rope like stalks, and its large fruits. They were native to tropical Africa and were introduced in India as decorative trees at different times by the British and perhaps even earlier by the Arabs. I even came to know that some of the photographs were of the tree from Calcutta, Bangalore, and Mandu! I was happy that my search was finally over.

Little did I know that my search was still incomplete! Last year, I went to the Indian Institute of Technology, Roorkee and was delighted to see a Sausage Tree in full bloom-long stalks of flowers hanging like decorated ropes. I told my host that I loved that tree. I boasted that it was Kigelia Africana or Sausage Tree! He smiled gently and pointed to the plaque near the base of the tree-Kigelia Pinnata! It took both of us, only a few minutes to check the internet and realize that both were accepted as the botanical names of the Sausage Tree!

I also did not know then that the Sausage Tree was to play an even bigger and sobering role in my life. Recently during a visit to Minnesota, while having black wild rice with turkey, during a Thanksgiving Dinner at a friend's house, I remarked that black rice was cultivated in Manipur, too. And then I told the guests about my visit there and also about the story of my discovery of the Sausage Tree.

One of the guests, an elderly and polite Japanese professor, approached me and took me aside. He took out a very old diary. It had belonged to his grandfather, he told. One of the last entries in that had described the long lines of tired, exhausted, and destitute Indians returning from Burma on foot and walking past his grandfather's tent near Imphal. His grandfather lay buried, there. His father was a student in Hiroshima and no trace was ever found of the hostel where he had lived to work for a Ph. D. He had no memory of his father or grandfather, though their photographs were preserved in the family. That diary was the only link he had with his elders. Both of us were greatly moved at this curious turn in our stories and felt close like brothers.

He requested me to describe the memorial for the Japanese. I told him what I could recall and added that, surprisingly, the place had exuded peace and tranquility, even though it was close to a highway with very heavy traffic. He requested me to send him photographs of the memorial, if I had any. I received his mail telling that he got the photographs, just this morning.

I wonder if his grandfather ever saw my grandfather,

walking in one of those long lines of Indians returning from Burma. If so, did he wonder about the irony of fate which brought one of them from a faraway land never to return and the other surviving a very long journey to return home from a faraway land, which the former had helped occupy? Could they have ever imagined that their grandchildren would meet one day in America?

The story of the journey of the Sausage Tree from Africa to Jammu, Mandu, Roorkee, Bangalore, Calcutta, and Manipur fills me with wonder. I also wonder that if one could read the coding of my genes, would it perhaps reveal the story of the journey of my ancestors from a tree in Africa to its savanna to Central Asia to Vastu Valley in Afghanistan to a remote village in North India.

What a wonderful story would that be!

9

This Canal Shall Speak No More

I wish this canal could speak again. And then I could talk to it about the days when an English man named Christopher organized its construction as a part of the Marhatta Ditch to surround the marsh which was to blossom into the city of Calcutta. And I could talk to it of the patrol boats which perhaps plied in it to provide security to this city. And I could ask it about the days when boats coming from Sunderban were repaired near Ultadanga-an island of inverted boats! And I could ask it about the days when the bheries of what was to become Salt Lake were drained into it, and when part of it was covered to make what we now know as Eastern Metropolitan Bypass.

My friend Bishuda, whose family has lived near Kankurgachi for many generations, tells me that when that happened, fish weighing many sers were sold for one to two annas each. How can a true blooded Bengali ever forget such a 'glorious' event. And finally I would have liked to ask it of the heroic efforts the East European engineers who converted the marshy land on its right bank into the township of Bidhan Nagar. However, this canal shall speak no more.

I first saw the Christopher Canal when I visited Bidhan Nagar twenty five years ago. I had come from Mumbai (which was Bombay then) to see my future place of work. I used the ferry which used to operate near Dum Dum Park on the Kazi Nazrul Islam Avenue, to cross it. I was new to Calcutta. It was only after startling many a taxi drivers by asking them to take me to Bidhan Nagar that I came to know that it was more popularly known as Salt Lake and that the Kazi Nazrul Islam Avenue existed only on the signboard near Ultadanga as the people preferred to call it the V. I. P. Road. Even the Christopher Canal was variously known as Krishnapur Khal and Kestopur Canal! I knew that Krishna could become Kesto in Bengal but I never understood how poor Christopher lost to Lord Kesto!

The water in the canal then was quite clear. I saw some fish swimming and many more buffaloes lounging in the canal-fully submerged with only their snouts peeping out of the water. Some urchins were also playing in the canal, reminding me of my childhood in a remote village in Eastern Uttar Pradesh.

I heard some amusing stories of the encounters of the buffaloes with the ferry. The one which I still remember was about the time when the ferryman did not notice a particular buffalo in the canal. The buffalo found itself beneath the ferry and did not like it. It stood up-the water was never too deep. The passengers in the ferry, first went up in the air and then joined the buffalo in the water. I understand that they had a good mud bath.

Many years later I got an apartment near the Kestopur Canal in Salt Lake. A road and a green strip separated us from the canal. A giant casuarina tree grew in front of our apartment. The highest branches came up to our seventh floor apartment and swayed even in the gentlest breeze.

By that time a new ferry ghat had started right in front of

our housing complex. It was convenient and added some spice to our lives. We would sit in the balcony and watch people crossing the canal in the ferry which was pushed across using a big bamboo stick. We would hear people laughing as the boat got filled up and swayed as it moved. In the morning farmers would come laden with vegetables. Fishermen came with baskets full of fish. Baskets full of clucking chicken would be loaded on the little ferry and brought to feed the people in Salt Lake. One would see cycles and motor bikes and even rickshaws ferried across.

The casuarina tree was full of green parrots and in the morning we would awaken to their concert. A neighbouring tree had quite a huge population of beaver birds. Yet another tree always had a big flock of bulbuls. During winter many birds from far away countries would alight in the canal and swim along, foraging for food.

During the night, we would often see jackals along the canal and sometimes inside our housing complex, playing like puppies in the sand heaped there for more construction. In the night we would often hear their calls, and I would tell my children that we called them 'Paharua'-calling after every prahar.

Often country boats laden with bamboos or earthen pots would go by, pulled by men by a rope, straining hard along the canal. Once in a while we would hear a phutphati going along.

During the rainy season, the water would often be muddy. Some children always played in the canal. Men often wallowed in the mud looking for fish. When our housing complex had a much smaller number of residents we even took the idols during

Saraswati Puja for immersion to the canal.

Yes, there was a time when this canal told us many tales.

A few years ago, pucca embankments were made. We saw the canal being dried and dug and cleaned. We would sit in our balcony and watch. At a number of points along the canal there were steps going down to the water. It all looked so grand.

Then a garbage dump was made near the canal. Cows from nearby khatal would scurry in the garbage throughout the day. Rag pickers would join them and pick pieces of plastic and paper and other valuables. The stench of rotting garbage became our constant companion. It would become unbearable when the trucks came to collect the garbage. But soon we got used to the smell and we do not notice it anymore, often even when the trucks come.

The pucca embankments on the canal have become a great beacon of hope. Many huts have come up along the canal. Little children play in the canal and women wash their clothes and their vessels even though the water is never clean. There have been cases of young women forcibly taken to its banks. I have not seen any fish swimming there. Buffaloes are not seen any more in Salt Lake. I doubt though, that they would have enjoyed a bath in the canal now. We still have many cows but they of course do not wallow in the canal.

The ferry man has made a bamboo bridge. He no longer ferries the people across. He just sits under a banyan tree collecting the 'toll' for crossing the bridge. That is a pity. I recall sitting in my balcony, reading 'Siddharth' by Hesse where a boatman ferries people across a river. I had looked up to a sight which had transported me to a realm of joy-not encountered often.

The canal is now often full of dark black water. The water hyacinth along the canal has survived and so have all the mosquitos. In the evening as you walk on the road along the canal they surround you in a huge envelop. We often see carcasses of dogs and cats floating in the canal. There are often vultures and crows pecking at them and taking a free ride as the carcass floats down. I remember a dead body floating face down and people looking and police coming to take it out. Who was he?

It has been a long time since I last saw a boat come from Sunderban, laden with bamboos or earthen pots. I have not heard the 'phutphati' either, for long. It has also been long since we last heard the call of jackals in the night.

Winter comes and goes by. None of the birds from the far away countries come to the canal any more. All the parrots left a few years ago and so did the beaver birds. One day the flock of bulbuls too flew away, never to come back.

But the casuarina tree is too strategically located. It has been requisitioned by a large family of crows who have made their nests in it. We often see the tree bending over precariously during Kal Baishakhi and yet somehow the nests remain intact.

We now wake up to an endless noise made by crows and rickshaws. When we go to the balcony, we see silent line of people crossing the canal on the bamboo bridge, their heads bent, and handkerchiefs on their nose.

And below their feet, the Kestopur Canal now full of dirty, black, stinking water flows by. And it does not tell any tales.

10

In Search of a Good Omen

My wife strongly believes that she can get me to lose weight by forcing me to go on a morning walk. Thus I am often forced to leave the cool (or the warm) comfort of my bed and go for a walk along the road which runs along the Kestopur Canal in Bidhan Nagar aka Salt Lake. I must admit that even though I do not like to be made to walk, I love this road.

Its charm starts at the Kestopur Kheyaghat, which is the name given to the crossing near a huge casuarina tree as not long ago we needed a ferry to cross the canal. But that was before the canal's bed was made "pucca" and the scores of huts came up along its banks. The footbridge, the shops and the rickshaws came much later. Now, of course, the canal is full of silt, water-hyacinth and jet-black stinking water where the kids of these huts bathe, the women wash their vessels and clothes, and the men make huge bundles of the plastic bags and bottles collected from garbage dumps and city roads. A green stretch separates you from this dehumanizing view as you walk along.

I meet a large variety of majestic trees and scores of birds of various descriptions- *bulbul*s, doves, parrots, *mynah*s, occasional *sonabau*s, ubiquitous sparrows and crows and of course the lovely squirrels and butterflies. And as I look up I see numerous kites gliding majestically along.

I also meet several persons who have paused to do a vigorous exercise or to say a prayer to the Sun, facing east. At one place some people have cleared a little ground and planted banana, *tulsi* and *mogra*s, and read from a religious book. And I come across maids rushing to their jobs, discussing the quarrels with their husbands and their employers. And I meet a band of giggling girls plotting escapades to meet their friends. I also meet several beautiful dogs walking their masters.

And I see the trees which the Forest Department of West Bengal has lovingly planted along the road and into the Deer Park and the green stretch beyond that. They have been very thoughtful and put their names on many of them. However, the spell is easily broken by advertisements of computer classes, coaching classes, mattresses, drivers and pizzas painted garishly and nailed to the trees. The trees display different facets of their charm as the season changes.

I love the *palash* trees, their leaves always three together with the touch of mildest yellow to the green, their flowers reminding me of beaks of parrots, their branches giving a feeling of rugged strength. And the *amaltas,* their yellow blossoms hanging like huge bunches of celestial grapes. And the gulmohar, its canopy stretching across the road, its flowers transforming the road below into a beautiful carpet and the tree above into a giant bouquet.

There are several trees of *jungle jalebi*, their fruits looking like beans swirling to make the *jalebi*s; *mynah*s and sparrows savouring its white and sweet pulp and its shining black seeds covering the road, growing into tiny versions of their mothers during rains and soon withering away. Only the blue bouquets offered by Jacarandas take away my sad thoughts. It also helps to know that the *akashmani*s will be in full bloom soon and their yellow flowers will fill the void created by the disappearing Peltophorems.

Just after the spring, the new leaves of *ashoka* change their colours quickly from translucent green-yellow-red-violet to dark green. Most of these trees are ungroomed and have branches growing haphazardly, each twisted or broken branch a repository of the *kalbaishakhis* which hit them. It is surprising that the trees hit by the storms somehow repair themselves within weeks but the lamp-posts destroyed by their fall can take several months to stand up again. And it is also surprising that while one of the dead trees in the Deer Park looks magnificent in the aftermath of death, the vehicles parked along the road for the last ten to fifteen years and rusting look uglier by the day.

By the end of April, the jack-fruit trees start getting their fruits which keep growing bigger and bigger till June or beyond. There is even a *jamun* tree in this stretch, whose flowers appear around April and the little green fruits soon after. By mid-June the fruits are luscious violet, scores of birds feed on them and people who still have some rusticity left in them pick up the fruits from the road, dust them and savour them. Surprisingly there are very few mango trees though a few neem trees growing at one end of the deer park have led to several neem saplings planted by crows feeding on their fruits.

There are several *sheesham* trees, and a fairly large *bel* tree, with its fruits decorating the branches and every leaf made immortal in the famous Bilva-stotram. There is a weeping willow, several Christmas trees, *kachanar*s, and huge sal trees.

On one of them a money plant climbs to a great height, its leaves more than a feet long with streaks of green and yellow splashed across them. The white-skinned eucalyptuses never fail to lend a mild fragrance to the breeze passing through them. One can, if one pays a close attention, listen to the rustling of the *peepal* leaves at one end of the road at any time of the day.

I am amazed at the numerous fig trees growing happily anywhere and everywhere, their large leaves sporting tiny `hairs' on them, their fruits covering every inch of their branches and a large number of rain trees, whose flowers cover the road during the peak of the summer.

The people living along this road have not remained unaffected by this bountiful display of mother-nature. Most of them have planted *harsingar*s, *rat-ki-rani*, *mogra* and *kamini* in the little stretch of land in front of their houses. In May and June, the *kamini* bushes are covered with snow-white blossoms and the ground beneath them is converted into a thick carpet of "virgin snow".

I wince as I see the servants use a broom to clean them out of the way for their masters to drive away. The lovely flowers are gathered in a corner where they struggle to maintain their grace in their dying moments.

I have walked long and now I can see the large stretch of the dirty canal, noisy traffic on the VIP Road, and a stretch of land covered with trees of castor oil seed. Beyond the magnificent *arjun* tree growing there, I see the rubbish produced by the building industry heaped along the canal and its smell assails me.

Let me return home. The *koel* is calling its mate and preparing the stage to give the job of rearing its chicks to the unsuspecting crows. Yes I should be back, along the "coolest road" which hides the ugly canal and the reality of life from me.

If I am in luck I will see a mongoose. And if the mongoose moves from my right to the left, I will know that I would have a nice day.

11

The Netherlands of Kolkata

Urdu poetry is truly sublime. And the life of some of the poets has been even more remarkable. One such Urdu poet is Basir Badr. It is believed that he is the only poet in the world of literature whose poetry was already included in the course work for master's degree when he rejoined his studies after a break due to financial hardship and he had to answer questions about it during his examinations. One of his famous couplets reads, "kuch to majbooriyan rahi hongi, yun hi koi bewafa nahin hota" (There must have been some difficulties/compulsions. No one turns unfaithful just like that). Any time I think of civic problems of Calcutta or Kolkata, this couplet comes to my mind.

People have been living continuously in Benaras for over 2000 years. Cities like Delhi or Allahabad are also quite old. I am talking about their continuation as a vibrant city and not as an occasional hut or hamlet. The city of Kolkata comes in the latter category.

It existed as three villages of fishermen, weavers, and the Goddess Kali- providing protection to robbers and dacoits. Till Job Charnock decided to turn it upside down. It went on to become The Paris of the East, The Jewel in the Crown, The City of Palaces and The City of Culture. The propensity to give it new names continues.

I have never understood the recent trend to call it "The City of Joy". In my humble opinion it only shows that we are adept at converting adversity into an opportunity and a curse into a praise. The book "City of Joy" by Dominique Lapierre describes a slum called Anand Nagar inhabited by lepers and beggars living in dehumanizing poverty. That name was translated as City of Joy.

Even the delightful phrase "Oh! Calcutta!" borrowed as the title of a long playing and controversial play and now a name of a delightful chain of restaurants is a pun on the French phrase "*O quelcult'as!*" which means, "what an ar.. you have!".

So where does the Urdu poetry quoted at the beginning feature in all this. Elementary. The average elevation of Kolkata, on the east of the Hooghly is just 17 feet above the sea level. Even the earlier Europeans settling around here shunned it and settled on the west of the river in what was to develop into Howrah. It has an average elevation of 39 feet above the sea level. Even then our ancestors called that land "hoar" which in Bangla stands for "a fluvial swampy lake", which- according to internet is,"sedimentologically a depression where water, mud and organic debris accumulate". No wonder our ancestors never considered it worthy of living and never settled there in large numbers. I wonder what name they had for the marshy land on the east of the river.

But courtesy Job Charnock and his *majboori*s or compulsions about which we do not have enough knowledge, except that the request of his compatriots to be allowed to settle on the west side of the river had been turned down by the

Moghul rulers of the time. And now, due to the haphazard developments, only occasionally planned half- nay quarter-heartedly, we are stuck with this city, which consisted of swamps and ponds and lakes and marshy land. These were drained, dried and covered with large buildings. And the process continues. But it is easy to fill a pond. However it is not easy to change the contour of a land which brought all the water from the surrounding areas which developed over centuries. The water as we all know is a liquid and the planet earth has a substantial gravity as discovered by Newton (or ancient Indians, if you wish not to offend our easily offended pride). Thus it flows and flows downwards, collecting at all those places where it had been collecting over centuries after falling from the skies. And yet we blame the municipal authorities for all our woes!

It was about fifteen years ago. We came to see our flat under construction on the VIP Road. It had rained heavily for days. In spite of the rains, the approach road was completely dry, the work was in full swing and there was no trace of accumulated water. There was a full bodied canal along the VIP Road, several large ponds brimming with water and a large number of trees. Over years, the canal has turned into a dirty drain clogged with plastic, garbage, silt, and dirty dark, stinking water. The ponds have transformed into hotels, shops, housings, hostels and the trees have vanished.

The area now gets water logged- with the slightest rains, forcing people to walk through knee deep or even waist deep water supersaturated with garbage from the roads, the spit, the excreta, the plastic bags, the rotting leaves, the silt, the bones, and all that you may or may not be able to imagine. The maids refuse to come, the office goers and school children wade across- their pants rolled up, their shoes in hands, the cars stall, SUVs struggle to ply producing large wakes behind them, and the rickshaw pullers charge a fortune to take you across the riviere! The situation prevails for days depending on the bounty from the skies. And it happens several times every year.

But does it have to be like this? A friend of mine, who is a golf enthusiast proclaims that there is no inappropriate weather for playing golf, there is only an inappropriate clothing. Thus we should know that there is no inappropriate place for building a house, there is only an inappropriate preparedness. After all a large part of The Netherlands is several feet below the sea level and is surrounded by the sea.

A long time ago the benefactor of Archimedes, King Hiero II asked him to design a luxury liner and a naval ship rolled into one. When ready, it could carry 600 people and was named Syracusia. It was perhaps the largest ship ever built in the days of antiquity. But it had a problem. Water used to get accumulated in its hold which had to be bailed out at regular intervals. Archimedes invented what is now known as Archimedes Screw to easily drain out the water. The screw became popular as a tool for lifting water from water bodies for irrigation across the world. Very recently, it was used to drain out water and sludge accumulated near the base of The Leaning Tower of Pisa and replace it with concrete to stabilize the tilt.

And The Netherlanders. They built dykes along the land and used the Archimedes Screw, propelled by their wind mills to drain out the water and even snatch a large chunk of land from the sea!

Our own Sunderbans are not far from Kolkata. The land there is also not too high above the mean sea level, they also often have dykes along their villages, but perhaps these are not very extensive and they definitely do not use the Archimedes Screw along with a wind mill to keep their land safe from the surrounding sea water.

But sooner or later we have to do it. The earth is getting warmer, the Arctic ice is melting, the sea level is rising, and our soothsayers are predicting drowning of a lot of coastal areas. Some people suggest that our beloved Kolkata would drown in the rising water. But it does not have to be that way.

Let us build dykes around our city and let us install Archimedes Screws to drain out water, during rains now and in times to come. The only requirement would be power to turn the screws! I wonder if the heat generated during the criticism of the civic authorities could be used for this.

Just think of the possibilities. We could rename our beloved city as The Netherlands of Kolkata. After all the Dutch came to the east even before the English. We could be correcting the history and obliterating the past, where the English reviled us for being what we have always been.

We could also create our own myths where a brave Apu would use his little finger to save the entire city from destruction. Or perhaps we could have a new avatar of Aruni-who lay on a bund to stop water from destroying the fields of his guru.

12

The Last Orchids

I was walking along The Mall with my children in Darjeeling when they pointed to the flowers "growing" on a tree along the road. We soon found out that several branches had orchids clinging to them, the way baby monkeys cling to the back of their mothers. Later we purchased some flowers and they stayed fresh in our room for the entire duration of our stay there. I returned to Kolkata and encouraged the gardener of our institute to try to cultivate some orchids. He was skeptical but bought several clumps and tied them to branches of different trees. Somehow the only ones to survive were the ones which were tied to a tree of bay leaves.

In course of time these prospered and every now and then we would be blessed with some flowers, though not in plenty as we had seen in Darjeeling. Whenever they blossomed I would walk up to the tree and marvel at their numerous roots clinging to the tree, their leaves smooth as velvet and their flowers in purple and white, with many purple dots in the stretch of white and white dots in the stretch covered by purple. Their delicate and intricate shape never failed to fascinate me. On some occasions there would be just one stem covered with just a few flowers which always saddened me.

I would often wonder about their original habitat and their

migration from country to country, ending up on a bay leaf tree in our garden. Unfortunately some years ago a severe cyclone which had devastated Orissa also strongly lashed our city for several hours. It uprooted the bay leaf tree and blew away the orchids growing on it. The tree-lined road in front of our institute was covered with uprooted trees and broken branches. Later I tried to persuade the gardener to get some orchids again but the entire tree cover of the institute was devastated and the small garden completely destroyed. He concentrated on recreating the garden by planting rapidly growing flowering plants like marigold!

The orchids were slowly buried deep in my memory, coming to the fore only occasionally when I saw their pictures or saw some poor specimen, coloured in deep blue ink like substance in shops, which never impressed me.

And then I took the Thai Air to go to San Francisco. There were orchids everywhere! At the check in counter, in the plane, even in the toilets. Just a few flowers on a single stem in thin and long test tubes of clear glass, but the effect was magnificent. They made my day. On my return I found a shop in South Calcutta which sold orchid flowers and if I ever went that way I would buy some, always being told not to waste money but with a smile by The Frau.

Then some years ago I went to Chhattisgarh. I hired a car to go on a long drive along a country road lined with huge mango trees on both sides. Suddenly I noticed tonnes of orchids blooming on the trees. The sun was shining gently. I asked the driver to stop. As I stood admiring them he called them useless as they had no smell and no one bought them or offered them to gods. I looked around. We were close to a coal belt and perhaps not too long ago the area was a thick forest. Perhaps those orchids had survived on the mango trees which were not cut down. I told him that those flowers could easily fetch ten rupees or more for each stem. He looked surprised but did not utter a word.

But I was not prepared for what happened next. Last year, I went to Chhattisgarh again and even travelled to Amarkantak through a reasonably thick forest along the same road and hired the same driver through the same friend who had arranged the drive for me earlier. When I was approaching the area where I had seen orchids on the earlier visit I asked the driver to slow down and asked my wife to be prepared for the spectacle of a "hanging garden" of orchids.

Alas! We saw none. There was no trace of the orchid plants! In pain I asked the driver if he knew of the fate of the flowers which used to grow on the trees.

'Oh yes', he replied. After dropping me back some years ago, he had returned with ladders and baskets and some people and had taken all the flowers to be sold in the neighbouring city. He had used the plants and their leaves as cushions, he added with pride. And then he told me with a glint in his eyes that he had made a lot of money by selling them!

I still curse myself for my innocuous comment which brought about the destruction of the orchids in the area which was perhaps once a lush green forest. The orchids were perhaps the last vestiges of the past when the land was full of trees and moisture and which was now covered with coal dust blowing from trucks carting the coal away.

A few months ago I had to go to Barasat to renew my driving license. The place was swarming with people and covered with dust. As I climbed to the first floor office for getting myself photographed I looked outside. I was amazed to see a huge "shirish tree" (rain tree). One of its major branches was completely dry while others were still somewhat alive with sparse leaves on them.

But they were covered with plants of orchids, like the ones I had seen in Chhattisgarh and which had taken roots on a tree of bay leaf in our institute.

I stopped to look closely to the annoyance of others coming from behind me. I noticed that none of the plants had any flower! I wondered if it was the wrong season. And then I remembered a saying that a "happy" orchid plant flowers throughout the year! What pain did they have? The dust? The noise? The dying tree? The lack of moisture? The relentless heat? Once again these looked like the vestiges of an era long gone when perhaps Barasat was full of trees.

For some time now, the trees along the VIP Road have been dying one by one and are being removed. This has brought the trees which used to be in the middle of the thick growth to the front, perhaps awaiting execution. A few days ago I noticed orchids growing on one of them. In fact there were several clumps. The leaves and even the glistening white roots holding on to the tree looked reasonably healthy but there were no flowers. Were the orchids not happy? Where did they come from? I did notice though that the tree was almost exactly across the Keshtopur Canal where the old bay leaf tree of our institute had stood a long time ago. Were he seeds transported from the orchids there?

Now I am afraid that the tree holding the orchids is also likely to be sacrificed on the altar of beautification, as several of its branches are dead and the remaining ones also have only sparse leaves.

I am also afraid that with that tree the lost orchids in our neighbourhood will also go. After all, an orchid growing on a tree and displaying its majestic, delicate, intricate, lovely flowers is a declaration to all that it is happy! But the fast new glitzy world has no use for them, except when they are kept in a flower vase in the drawing room.

13

And Then the Wind Died

As our bus going towards airport would cross the little bridge over the canal at Ultadanga, the driver would press the accelerator pedal to the floor, the helper would bang the sides of the door with his bare hands and yell at the top of his voice-leaning more than half out of the door, his shirt buttons open-down to his belly. The cool wind would hit us all, but the best would be reserved for the helper. The fresh air would balloon his shirt, hit his face and blow through his hair. In a split second he would forget all the quarrels he had had with passengers, pedestrians, other bus drivers, rickshaws, tram drivers, taxi-drivers and the police. He would also forget the bad and congested roads and the crawling traffic. The journey to the airport from Ultadanga used to last just about twenty five minutes or less.

But it was enough to make us all relaxed and shed our stresses. Forgotten would be the long hours of hard work, hot, smelly, congested rooms of our offices, and the frequently failing electricity. Also forgotten would be roads covered with potholes, excessive noise of people yelling, police shouting, buses and taxis honking, and smelly sweating passengers and sweltering heat even during the peak of summer.

And the journey in the other direction in the morning was

enough to give us strength to face the day.

The journey was along the Kazi Nazrul Islam Avenue, a name which hardly any one used in spite of the huge popularity of the poet. The road was more popularly known and continues to be known as the VIP Road. The stretch from Ultdanda to airport had about 3 lanes each, for the up and down traffic. The minibuses and buses were the lords of the road, moving at ultra-legal high speeds, as if in a hurry to reach but actually to maximise the feeling of the wind in the face.

And what a wind and what a view the road offered! On both sides of the road, there were huge flowering and other evergreen trees. A gentle canal flowed along the right, moving away at Kestopur and replaced by tree lined water bodies, mostly ponds. At any time of the day, till almost dusk one would see women bathing, children playing, washer-men washing clothes and occasionally buffaloes lounging in them.

And the trees. The eucalyptuses outgrew them all, their barks glittering milky white and a faint smell of their whitish-green leaves pervading the air surrounding us. And the majestic gulmohars (Delonixregia) - the whole tree covered with red flames during spring, the green leaves completely obscured by the flowers. One wonders whether the phrase "Dhagaddhagaddhagajjwalallalatapattapavake" (brilliant flames of fire cover His face) of Tandava Stotra attributed to Ravana was inspired by a tree like this, so lovingly called the Flame of Forest. Or should one be swayed by their christening as Krishnachuda, their brown trunks draped in a flowing red silk dhoti of flowers. In the morning, while going to work, one could see the land underneath them covered with a lovely carpet of petals, blazing red, with a tinge of yellow at the edges, extending to almost the middle of the road.

And how could anyone separate Radha from Krishna? So one had so many Radhachudas (copper pod or Peltophorum pterocarpum) trees covered with bright yellow flowers, immortalized by so many poets and folk-singers in the yellow saree worn by Radha, their smell mingling with many other smells. Several jarul (Lagerstroemia speciosa or Pride of India) trees spotted the road on both sides complete with their lovely light violet flowers in spring and bunches of fruits later. And how can one forget the innumerable saptaparni (Alstoniascholaris or chhatim) trees which gave out such soothing smell when covered with the white bunches of flowers and had such lovely leaves. Why should people call it the Indian Devil Tree?

As spring approached we had flowers of palash (Butea monsperma) bright orange red, which reminded us of the approach of the Holi and Doljatra. Even when the summer was at its peak, the sky rained fire, the tar on the road melted, and even the birds took shelter in the trees, the giant shirish trees (Albizia lebbek or the rain tree) provided a cool sight to our eyes, their flowers, like micro-fountains of shining fibres in greenish white or violet near the base and getting much lighter as they approached the end. While the leaves glistened dark green in the morning, they would fold and go to sleep as the sun went down, their flowers continuing till early monsoon started drenching us. A touch of exotic was provided by occasional jacaranda with their purple blue flowers and African Tulips with their blood red ones.

A little later the scores of kadamba (Neolamarckia cadamba) trees with their large glassy leaves would be adorned with golden laddu like flowers peeping shyly and yet proudly from behind the leaves. The parrots and doves flew from tree to tree, eating freely from scores of jungle jalebis (Pithecellobium dulce) and sitting momentarily on amaltas trees (cassia fistula) covered with bunches of flowers hanging like celestial golden grapes.

Even the undergrowth was so lush green and varied! The tallest undergrowth was of lusty eranda (Ricinus communis or castor oil plant) with its large leaves, starting as dark reddish purple when young and then becoming dark shiny green when mature, growing closely. I had even seen a thick undergrowth of tulsi (Ocimum tenuiflorum or holy basil) plants in one stretch there. The rainy season and later was the best time for the creepers to cover the trees with their growth. They climbed even the electricity poles and brought back memories of Bhartrihari who famously (mischievously?) commented that creepers and kings get attached to whosoever is near them. I do not have courage to mention the third living being named by him, i.e., women, for fear of being lynched. By late winter or early spring many of the creepers would flower, covering the trees with multi-coloured flowers of all shapes and sizes. The wild kundru (Cocciniagrandis, telakucha, or bimba) creepers would also be in full bloom and get heavy with green fruits which would slowly turn bright red, immortalised by Kalidas in the phrase "pakvabimbadharosthi" (having lips like ripe bimba fruits).

There were clusters of gular trees (Ficus racemose), their trunks sprouting clusters of fruits, slowly maturing into velvety violet and being fed upon by large size ants and various birds. One could also see clusters of madar or aak (Calotropisprocera) plants with their leaves which had coated themselves with talcum powder, their flowers white and light violet, their fruits like a green croissant, their seeds flying around on the wings of their feathery white hairs

Every now and then we had pipal (Ficusreligiosa) trees of various ages, their leaves shining and swaying, bestowing peace and tranquillity upon all, their branches giving shelter to birds and unseen spirits. One could often see clay idols of Shitala on Her Donkey, deposited near their trunks.

Of course there were so many trees of neem (Azadirachtaindica) and semal (Bombaxceiba or cotton tree), their leaves turning translucent light red to dark green, and then tuning yellow, before falling in showers with the passage of time. The sheesham (Dalbergiasissoo) trees had their own cycle of green leaves turning light green and then grey, before falling. The trees when laden with pods, relished by monkeys had a charm of their own.

The first to go were the water bodies. It started slowly, almost imperceptibly and seemingly innocently. Every now and then some garbage would be dumped at their edge. Slowly the water started stinking, children and women stopped bathing there and the washer-men stopped using them. Gone were the rows of clean clothes hanging on ropes and fluttering in the wind. As the water-bodies were slowly chocked, first a road and then houses came up at their place. The bend in the canal near Kestopur became a cluster of huts where huge piles of scrap collected by rag-pickers started getting accumulated.

The large shirish trees were the next to go. Something happened and one by one they shed all their leaves and died, their bark peeled off and revealed the white dead trunks which turned to grey-black with time. The others followed the suit and one by one most of the large trees were gone.

The Kestopur Canal was dredged and the soil rich in toxic waste of the city was deposited upon the undergrowth killing it completely. The trees struggled to survive, often losing their limbs and branches to faceless hackers. The birds mostly vanished or moved away.

Now as I travel along the VIP Road, I see heaps of rubbish, stinking and full of broken bricks, garbage, broken wash basins and commodes of china, broken tiles, chunks of concrete, lifeless and depressing on which nothing, not even a blade of grass, grows.

And, for quite sometime now, while travelling along the VIP Road, I close my eyes and try to imagine, just how beautiful was my daily journey.

And the helpers of the buses do not feel the wind in their face any more.

14

The Abandoned

This is a very simple tale. It has no dramatic twists and no divine interventions.

It is just a tale of two children- both abandoned at birth.

One is sold to a kotha (a dance house) and is trained to be a courtesan. However, changing times reduce her to a dancing girl.

The other is found by a rich farmer, who raises him as a slave in return for leftover food, discarded clothes and a corner in his cattle shed to sleep.

The first child goes through a grueling training to be a mujra dancer and a singer par excellence. She learns the etiquettes of a courtesan and the circumstances force her to warm the beds of influential and rich. She finds solace in her music.

The other essentially invents music by making a flute for himself and slowly and painstakingly learns to play it well and finds solace from it in the middle of back-breaking work and continuous pain and humiliation about his birth and his sinning mother.

Then they meet- as in fairy tales and rejoice briefly in each other's company.

But only too briefly, unlike in fairy tales.

When I heard this story from Dr. Sharma, I told him that it seemed to revolve around some iconic folk songs adopted by the Hindi film industry. He smiled wisely and added that we should not be such snobs and shrug our shoulders to reality- these songs are extremely popular as they reflect the 'joie de vivre' as well as the deep anguish and helplessness of our people and they have given solace to millions for decades in their struggle for survival. I did not argue further with him.

However, the above prologue does not convey anything. It does not tell whether Putli Bai was abandoned and dumped in a garbage bin because she had an unmarried or a long widowed mother or she was just an unwanted female child. Be as it may, but she definitely had an uncaring, selfish and cowardly father, who had perhaps invented an excuse of "many compulsions" to silence his own conscience- if he had any, and left her mother to face the consequences. We would never know.

Putli Bai escaped extreme misery and a certain death, right after her birth, but for the sweeper who spotted her- before the stray dogs could devour her and took her to the locality of courtesans. He had frequented it often, with similar bundles of female babies in the past and returned with some money in his pocket. He was confident of the good money he was likely to earn as the baby was in good health. It also had sharp features and a fair complexion. He had made such visits for years. And before him, his father had done the same and so had his grandfather. And they had kept the supply chain for the locality alive for as long as one could remember. Should they have left these babies to be killed by stray dogs? Who are we to judge?

They could not have taken them home as they already had too many mouths to feed.

It also does not tell that Bahetu was most probably born of an unmarried or a long widowed mother, as normally people do not abandon a male child. One would never know whether his mother was taken forcibly or she was duped by someone promising to marry her and then walking away, as cowards have done for centuries all over the world.

Let us get back to the story that Dr. Sharma told.

Chaudhuri had found him lying in the ravine, wrapped in a bundle of dirty clothes. On a closure look, he had seen that the baby was still alive and in fact fast asleep. A new-born male child abandoned in the wild ravine, frequented by wolves, jackals, foxes and stray dogs, pointed to an unmarried or a long-widowed mother. In fact the wild animals would have surely killed him, if he was left there. Chaudhuri had hesitated at first. And then a thought had occurred to him. He had picked up the child and brought him home.

His wife had created a scene and shouted, "Whose sin have you brought home?"

He had just grunted, "Do you know how much we have to pay to our workers? He will survive on the leftovers and grow up to be a helping hand for life, for free", and ordered her to look after him.

His wife had understood the logic and yet with feigned reluctance and disgust, she had agreed to keep him.

Their youngest child was about ten years old and she along

with her older siblings rejoiced at having a baby to play with. They named him Bahetu ("the abandoned"). He survived under the loving care of the young girl. As he became older, he followed her like a puppy as she offered the only protection from cruel children of the neighbourhood and even her older brothers, who enjoyed pinching and slapping him, whenever they found him alone.

By the time he was about seven years old, his guardian was married away. He was never to see her again as Chaudhuri, on some pretext or the other, never invited his daughter to even visit him.

The day Chaudhuri's daughter left, his few clothes were thrown into a corner of the cattle shed and he was asked to move there. Bahetu had cried his heart out as she had left with her husband. He had refused to eat for two days. He was brutally kicked in the ribs by Chaudhuri's wife to stop shedding tears and start working- whether he ate or not.

That kick changed his life in an instant. No one was to see him laugh or even smile for a very long time to come.

As Bahetu had grown older, he had heard the story of his being abandoned by his "cruel, selfish and sinning" mother in the ravine, every day. The children of the neighbourhood had often ganged up against him, chanted ditties which described his mother as a sinning whore and thrashed him mercilessly whenever they found him alone without any pretext.

However, Bahetu never cried. He had already realized that there was no one to console him. He ate the leftovers of the children of Chaudhuri, wore their discarded clothes, did whatever he was ordered to do- and he was ordered around a lot, and attained years. Did he ever compare his own plight with those of the children of Chaudhuri? We do not know, as he never uttered a word about it.

Chaudhuri had already asked Bahetu to start taking care of his cattle. He was a rich farmer, with several pairs of oxen, cows and buffaloes. The person looking after the cattle was put on some other job.

Bahetu awoke to a shout from Chaudhuri or his wife- very early in the morning and was immediately put to work. He got buckets of water from the well and fodder from the barn for all the cattle. Then he cleared the cow dung, carrying it to the dung-heap. He was still too young with small hands and little strength. He could carry only half a bucket of water and only half a basket of fodder, necessitating numerous trips. It took him a lot longer to finish even simple jobs. And all along Chaudhuri would be shouting, abusing, boxing his ears, thrashing him often and cursing him to move quickly. He was almost always joined by his wife who egged him on and complained about the amount of food Bahetu consumed and how he never did anything.

It would be almost nine by the time he finished. He would look blankly as he saw all the children of the village go to school. It was also the time when he was asked to go and eat the leftovers of the children of Chaudhuri.

Let us digress a little to tell what one means by leftovers. We shall use it for want of a better word. In fact there is no equivalent of the Hindi word "juthan" in English. It stands for the half-eaten food, like chapatti or rice or dal, which is left in the plate after someone has finished eating. In earlier days, sweepers and mushhars (men who killed and ate mice) went from house to house- especially in semi-rural areas, collecting this juthan, which would otherwise have been thrown to animals. Upper class Hindus would not eat juthan of any one- not even of those from their own family. "Unclean" is more like it. But we shall continue to use leftovers for the ease of usage.

Let us get back. So, by this time, the workers for the fields of Chaudhuri would have taken the oxen to work in the fields. And even before Bahetu hurriedly wolfed down his food, Chaudhuri and his wife would be hollering for him with a list of domestic chores, like cleaning the vast courtyard, sprinkling water, moving things about etc.

And then he took the cows and the buffaloes to the ravine- which led to the river and the forest for grazing with a small bundle of leftover chapattis, an onion and a few chillies. He could be seen passing the spot where he was found every day and stopping momentarily and then staring blankly at some point beyond the horizon.

He ate the chapattis with chillies and raw onion and drank water from the river- along with the cattle, talking to them, washing them in the river and driving them to better pastures.

As the sun set, he brought the cattle back to their shed, tethering them to their stakes. By this time the workers would return with the oxen and he had to run to get water and fodder for them. After every one had eaten, Chaudhuri's wife would shout for him and throw the leftovers at him to eat.

This was to be his routine for almost fifteen years. There is a saying in our parts of the world that "the fate of even dung-heaps changes for the better after twelve years". Bahetu's fate was obviously much worse.

When it rained, he would go to the forest and return with a large basket of grass. He would mix it to the chaff or other fodder along with mustered oil cakes or mahua oil cakes soaked overnight in water along with dried flowers of mahua to be given to the animals.

The animals loved him. They would start bellowing and mooing as he approached and jostled with each other to get his attention as he poured water or fodder into their manger. The oxen of Chaudhuri were known to be ferocious and had chased and hurt quite a few persons in the village. But they were very gentle with him. He would often stand there, gently rubbing the dewlap of the cows and the backs of oxen, and talking softly to them. The cattle responded by nudging him playfully. And he slept in a bundle of hay spread in a corner in the cattle shed.

As years passed, other duties were thrust upon him. Every once in a while one of the ploughmen would not turn up and he would go and work in the fields. During the winter he helped irrigate the fields of wheat and during summer he was asked to help with the irrigation of sugarcane fields and tobacco. And during night, he was asked to guard the fields against the invasion of neelgais, wild pigs, porcupines and a stray bull or a stray he-buffalo- belonging to no one in particular and drifting from one place to other and chased by all.

He could be seen wearing a torn dhoti and a vest with many holes of different sizes, during all the months- blazing summer, wet rains and cold winter. Festivals had no meaning for him. Rest did not have any meaning for him either- as the moment he was spotted sitting down, he was hauled up to carry out some other work.

Then one day seeing children playing with flutes which they had bought from the city fare, he made a flute for himself by looking at one of the flutes which the kids had thrown away. He had time to experiment when he took the cattle to graze and discarded many before settling on one that he had made by burning holes in a bamboo stick. And he taught himself to play the flute.

He had earlier experimented a little with two pairs of discarded plough-shares, held in his palms and shaken together to produce music. However, he found them to be too loud, occasionally screechy and limited in range and richness and had given up. The flute had infinitely many possibilities.

He improved painstakingly slowly but rejoiced in the small stretches of melodies he could produce. He listened closely to the folk musicians who came to the village with marriage parties or during functions or just passed by and improved slowly. This gave him immense happiness. No one could remember to have seen him smile in earlier times. Yet, now when he drove the cattle to the ravine and beyond, he could be seen smiling occasionally as he made clicking sounds to get them close.

Slowly he learned to play the flute so well that people could easily make out the song he was playing from the tunes. Once in a while, he was asked by people to play for them. And he always obliged. As he was getting popular, but never neglecting the cattle and never showing even a slightest reluctance to do any job he was asked to do, never ever reacting to insults and abuses and curses, even Chaudhuri's wife- who had never ever displayed any tender feelings for him, started grudgingly behaving a little less harshly with him. This meant that instead of throwing the leftover half-eaten chapattis at him from a distance, she dropped them in his aluminum plate or outstretched palms.

Chaudhuri had become the village chief by now and was busy minting or rather milking money from many of the welfare schemes being implemented by the government. His mud house had been replaced by a brick house with a large courtyard and a shed for cattle.

The oxen had been sold and replaced by a tractor which was parked in one corner of the cattle shed. He had increased the number of buffaloes and milking the cows and buffaloes had become a part of Bahetu's duty. The wife of Chaudhuri kept a hawk's eye upon him as he milked the cows and buffaloes as she could never trust that he was not stealing the milk. Of course, every day she threatened to throw him out of the house if she ever came to know of it, after breaking his hand and feet and throwing him back to place from where Chaudhuri had picked him up. There was no reason for Bahetu to believe that she would not carry out her threat.

Chaudhuri personally supervised the addition of water to the milk, before it was loaded on to the tractor and sent to the neighbouring city for sale.

On one occasion Bahetu had tripped and spilled some milk. It had led to a very harsh thrashing by Chaudhuri and denial of food to him for two days. Doubling over with hunger and fatigue, he had continued to work as usual and lived only on water. In fact he was denied food on one pretext or the other and leftovers were given to the family dog or the cattle, as he looked.

On such occasions, he had just watched stoically and in silence, looking blankly at some point beyond the horizon. Chaudhuri and his wife were convinced that these punishments and regular insults were necessary to keep him under control.

Why did he not run away? We do not know. Perhaps, as someone had remarked once, he was living out the punishment meted out to him for his deeds in a previous birth.

Around this time Chaudhuri decided to get his eldest grandson married. The fellow had some kind of a job in the city. That, along with the overall prosperity of Chaudhuri ensured a good marriage with an ample dowry. In order to give a demonstration of his wealth, Chaudhuri decided to get one of the famous dancing girls from the city to accompany the marriage party. He personally travelled to the city and gave her "saee" (earnest money) confirming the invitation. She arrived a day earlier and Chaudhuri decided to have a performance from her, on the night before the marriage party was to leave for the bride's place.

Putli Bai was young, very pretty, sang extremely well and danced even better. Her party of musicians accompanied her on tabla and sarangi. The elder courtesan, who had purchased her from the sweeper was rather advanced in years for the profession and was reduced to the status of adviser, guardian, secretary, accountant and house-manager rolled into one according to the traditions of her locality and profession. She sat along with the party of the musicians, perhaps thinking of the days when she used to give performances to a lot lesser rowdy bunch of people. She had already started contemplating getting a child to train for the time when Putli Bai would be old. After all, it took years to prepare them for the job.

As the evening progressed, several Petromax lamps filled the venue- a gaily covered shamiana (a flat tent, open on all sides) with shining white sheets spread over soft carpets, with a glittering light. The villagers, in their best clothes, sat on the sheets-leaning against soft round pillows. A man sprinkled rose-water on them from a shining silver sprinkler. Hookahs with scented tobacco were passed around. Another helper took a plate full of cotton buds dipped in itr (perfume) and people took one or two buds each to rub them gently on the inside of their wrists and to tuck them behind their ears. Some of them had little garlands of mogra flowers wrapped around their wrists. Several plates, loaded with dry fruits, pan (betel leaf with chips of areca nut and fragrant spices) and cigarettes were also doing rounds. A few strong men were discreetly stationed near-by to handle men, if they became unruly or left their seats to get close to the dancer.

Putli Bai, in her vibrant colourful silk sari, glittering gold ornaments, youthful looks- with only the mildest make up, confident erect posture, palms and forearms covered with intricate designs using henna, tinkling and shining glass bangles interspersed with diamond studded gold bangles reaching almost up to her elbows, a near translucent fair complexion-accentuated by a touch of talcum powder, her cheeks additionally flushed with a touch of rouge, long lustrous dark hair braided with a garland of fragrant mogra flowers, an intoxicating perfume, full red lips, shining white uniform teeth, sharp features, dark kohl lined eyes and manicured and gaily polished nails looked like a celestial nymph to the villagers. They were used to their drab and rustic women-their rough and callus covered hands with broken and dirty nails, smelling of dirt and cow dung, their weather-beaten rough feet, their entangled, dirty, dry and smelly hair, their sun-burnt skin and their faces covered with a veil at all times.

Women of the village assembled in the verandah of Chauduri's house behind a thin curtain and whispered about her looks and manners, giggling and shying at the effect she was having on their men folk.

Putli Bai sat in the middle, deliberately slowly tying her ankle bells on her feet covered with vibrant designs in alta (a deep red water colour) while the musicians tuned their tabla and sarangi.

The performance began. The music and the lilting voice of Putali Bai could be heard clearly in the silence of the night. Bahetu listened attentively from his corner in the cattle shed. Every song, every beat, every tune was getting etched in his mind.

He got only an occasional glimpse of Putli Bai as she whirled around to escape the outstretched hands of the people-with money in them, yet collecting the money deftly without allowing them to touch her. He sat transfixed.

The function continued till late night. In the morning, Bahetu got up and as usual milked the cows and buffaloes. Then he tied the leftover food which Chaudhuri's wife gave him in a piece of cloth and gathered his herd of cattle to take them for grazing.

As he reached the edge of the houses he took out his flute and slowly started playing the tune of one of the songs he had heard. It was a famous song:

"O' Beloved, I beseech you,

Do not take the path through the ravine and the river."

Line by line, he played the entire song on his flute, imagining that Putli Bai was singing only for him.

Putli Bai was still asleep, exhausted from her previous evening's exertions. She dreamt of a very soft and soothing music coming from afar and woke up with a start. She awakened the musicians and the old courtesan, asking them to listen. The music was drifting away. She asked them to find out who was playing the flute. The eagerness of villagers longing to gossip provided them all the details.

Bahetu had been asked to return by noon- for the first time as far as he could remember, to help with the preparations of the marriage party. He returned playing another one of the songs which Putli Bai had sung the previous night:

"What is the tinkling of my anklets trying to tell you, again and again?

O' Beloved, I get restless without you."

He stopped abruptly as he approached the houses.

As soon as he tethered the cows and the buffaloes in the cattle shed, he was pressed into the service of the marriage party getting ready to leave. He ran around, getting them water, food, their clothes, their boxes, their other belongings. Oblivious to him, Putli Bai was keeping a close eye on him. The marriage party was almost ready to leave.

Putli Bai approached Chaudhuri and asked him to lend her a labourer to help her with her boxes of dresses and musical instruments.

And then, almost innocently and very casually, she pointed to Bahetu, who was running with a bucket of water for someone's bath and asked Chaudhuri, "Who is he? He looks like a servant? Could he come with us?" Chaudhuri was hassled with myriad other problems and without paying any attention agreed.

Bahetu was called to Putli Bai. She looked at his dust and mud covered legs, his matted hair, his unkempt beard, his torn dhoti, his vest with a million holes, at the bare sole of his feet-covered with cracked thick leathery skin and his dark and innocent bewildered eyes. He looked at her only once and then hastily lowered his eyes to the ground. She asked someone to get a barber who gave him a haircut and a shave. She gave him a cake of scented soap and asked one of her musicians to help him with a scrubbing bath and also to give him a change of clothes and one of their shoes. He returned with Bahetu in clean clothes, shoes, trimmed moustache and a turban. She looked at him and her heart missed not one but several beats. Bahetu did not lift his head.

And then he heard her dulcet voice asking him to get his flute.

He sat on the decorated bullock-cart with her party almost in a trance. She told him that she had come to know that he played flute very well. When he blushed, she added that she was going to call him Murali (flute) and not Bahetu, till he was with her.

The world had changed for Bahetu in just a few hours. And now the only thing that he owned- his name, was also being taken away from him. The events had moved so fast that he had not even been able to make arrangements for the cattle. Putli Bai told him not to worry about them. Was he upset? We would never know, for he never uttered a word to anyone about this.

The marriage went very well. No one paid any attention to Bahetu who had been supposedly pressed into the service of Putli Bai. During the night, when her dance recital started, Chaudhuri and other villagers were surprised to find him sitting with the musicians in a clean dress.

The performance of Putli Bai was picking up. She first sang a hymn and a blessing for the well-being of the bride and the groom. Then she sang a paean to the generousity of the Chaudhuri house-hold. She started to sing a gazal. Almost immediately there was a chorus demanding that she sing the famous song, "Do not take the path through the ravine and the river". She feigned surprise and consented- coyly.

The tabla and the sarangi kept pace with her singing, her movements, her acting, her coming close coquettishly to the people and dancing away, her whirling as she deftly took the bills from their outstretched hands and touched her forehead with them to signal gratitude and appreciation and deposited them with the musicians and the elder courtesan. Her ankle bells and glass bangles produced a music of their own in perfect tune with the tabla and the sarangi. Bahetu looked spellbound at her- as if she was imploring "him" not to go to the ravine with Chaudhuri's cattle, which he had done- day after day for so many years.

Chaudhuri had earlier pointed out the important guests to Putli Bai. She in turn while dancing went near them- one by one, and half-kneeled in front of them. Then she pulled her saree gently over her head and holding it delicately between the fingers of her two hands and made a kind of yawning over her face. She continued to sing, gently tapping her feet to the rhythm of the music and occasionally bit a corner of her lowers lips and blinked her eyes several times, smiling coyly and acting as if she was bewitched by their charm. They rewarded her amply for which she thanked them again by touching the money to her forehead and danced away, never ever missing a beat.

As the dance progressed- before anyone could realize, Bahetu took his flute out and started playing the song on it. Putli Bai was surprised. She stood still for a full second and then started performing even more majestically, even more seductively, even more suggestively. People were showering her with money and urging her to go on and on. She was getting utterly exhausted and gave a hint to the musicians to stop. Slowly they brought the piece to a conclusion and she flapped down, giddy with success, gratitude and satisfaction.

After a little rest she started again and on this occasion, Bahetu or rather Murali accompanied her from the very beginning. He was doing so well that the other musicians stopped for some time. This brought out the sweetness of his flute, the near-perfection and the soulful long stretches of his recital to the fore. The musicians were quite experienced and improvised to keep pace with his untutored, unstructured and wild wonderings. Putli Bai had never ever made so much money in one evening. She continued to perform and Bahetu continued to play well beyond the midnight to almost early hours of the morning and her companions continued to collect the money.

She was to return to the city later that day. She approached Chaudhuri to take his leave. Chaudhuri was in a very happy frame of mind. He was very pleased with the whole affair. The arrangements for the wedding had been extravagant, he had collected a huge dowry and the performance of Putli Bai was a huge success. After some pleasantries, she asked Chaudhuri to take Bahetu with her as she desperately needed a helping hand.

Chaudhuri was taken aback. He had never paid any serious attention to Bahetu, except when he had picked him up from the ravine or when he had felt it necessary to curse him. Even during the dance performances of Putli Bai, he was too drunk to have noticed anything. However he knew the amount of work Bahetu was doing in return for a corner in the cattle shed, leftovers, and discarded clothes. Yet, for some time he had been thinking of getting rid of the cows and the buffaloes as there were frequent checks of the milk he was supplying and only a hefty regular bribe to the officials was allowing him to make a large enough profit.

He made a great show of having brought up Bahetu as "his own son" and how much his wife and children loved him and cared for him during sickness and injuries. He told that they never ate without feeding him, provided the best clothes to him and he was pupil of their eyes.

Putli Bai, who had received a good training in dealing with rich and powerful, kept quiet, smiled sweetly and repeated her request- even more politely. The greed of Chaudhuri was taking shape. He blurted that Bahetu's leaving would cause them a great loss. After some haggling, he agreed to let Bahetu go and "take up a job with her", in return for twenty thousand rupees immediately and a monthly pay of two thousand rupees every month to be sent to Chaudhuri. It was a huge sum. Putli Bai agreed.

They returned to the city.

Putli Bai got a tutor for Murali, as she insisted on calling Bahetu. The tutor was pleasantly surprised to notice the natural talent of Murali. He got a proper flute for him and started from the basics of the grammar of the music. Bahetu proved to be a very keen student and quickly picked up even the minutest details of the most popular ragas which Pulti Bai loved. Slowly and painstakingly, the tutor identified and removed the rough edges from the music of Bahetu and after some time he started regularly accompanying Putli Bai during dances in weddings and other functions or at the mujras she performed at her kotha.

For the first time in his life he was sleeping in a bed, wearing new clothes, and eating fresh meals with the rest of them and he was being treated as one of them. In return, he poured his soul into the flute.

Whenever Putli Bai got up to sing and dance, he closed his eyes to the world and the people lusting after her and imagined that she was singing for him and only for him and his flute rejoiced in her love. The combined effect of all this had a mesmerizing effect on the audiences and they reciprocated in ample measure, in the only way they knew- showering her with money.

The life had become good, very good.

By now he had fallen madly in love with Putli Bai. To anyone looking it was quite clear that she was also quite fond of him and genuinely cared for him. Was she in love with him too? We shall see.

She often talked of finding a "good girl" to get him married and to settle him in a house of "his own", so that "he could die in peace". Murali used to get quite baffled by all this as she was very young and he had realized that she had also started loving him greatly.

Putli Bai was a courtesan. But the good, old, cultured ways of courtesans were almost gone and all of them had been reduced to dancing girls. Quite often she was also obliged to tolerate and satisfy the lustful advances of her rich clients and high government officials. However, Bahetu used to get very baffled that she never allowed him to get even slightly intimate with her.

One evening after a long and very fulfilling performance, Putli Bai made a present of a silver flute to him. He played several songs on the flute till early morning, with Putli Bai listening to him, a smile on her face.

Their fame had, by then, spread far and wide and invitations for their performances were multiplying so rapidly that Putli Bai was forced to decline quite a few.

They had returned from yet another performance. Putli Bai was resting. The other musicians had left. The older courtesan had gone to Lucknow to buy some dresses etc. Murali went to the room of Putli Bai and stood watching. The strands of the music they had played during the performance were still ringing in his mind. Her long tresses partially covered her face. He sat by her side and gently moved them aside. He realized that he had never touched her till then. His felt his heart-beats rise and started breathing heavily.

Putli Bai whispered something softly in her sleep, a smile lit her face, and she turned a bit. Murali leaned on her. Still deep in her sleep, Putli Bai clasped him in her arms.

Almost immediately, she awoke with a start and threw him off her chest.

He was quite baffled as she sat sobbing hysterically, hitting his chest with her fists, holding him tightly and pushing him away all at the same time. It was then that he understood.

In a flash he realized why she had never let him even touch her, even though she had developed a deep love for him. He understood, why she had always talked about getting him married to a "good girl" and "settling him in a house" away from her.

He realized that the only person who had ever loved him had also struggled hard to see that he did not drink from the poisoned chalice that she had become.

✼ ✼ ✼

Putli Bai's sickness was far more advanced than they had realized. Bahetu, the musicians and the old lady struggled to nurse her, forcing her to take her medicines regularly, forcing her to eat, trying to keep her amused. Her performances had reduced considerably.

Once in a while she would ask Bahetu to play his flute for

her. Bahetu would close his eyes, imagine her singing and dancing and play. Sometimes the musicians accompanied him, even as Putli Bai was strongly advising them to find employment elsewhere. During all this they had forgotten to send money for three months.

Chaudhuri sent his son to find out.

I had been treating Putli Bai for some time. I slowly came to know the story of Bahetu from him. That day Bahetu had come to my clinic to collect medicines for her. I noticed the signs of the sickness in him and advised him to undergo some tests and to start taking medicines, before it was too late.

Around the same time, Chaudhuri's son had arrived at the kotha, climbed the flight of stairs to the floor above, pushed the musicians aside and entered the room of Putli Bai. She was running a mild fever. Seeing him, she asked the elder courtesan to hand over three month's "salary" to him.

Perhaps he had his eyes for Putli Bai from the time when she had danced at the wedding. Perhaps, he had found that her complexion had turned even fairer due to the anemia which had already started affecting her. Or, perhaps, he was excited by looking at her cheeks- flushed due to the fever. Or, perhaps, he knew that he was son of Chaudhuri and she was just a dancing girl, whose job was to entertain him. He tried to pull her towards himself, insisting on getting the "interest for the delayed payments". She screamed. The musicians came running. But they were no match for him.

By then Bahetu had returned. Hearing the commotion, he

had rushed to the upper floor of the house and entered the room of Putli Bai. She was shaking with fear and anger and stood in a corner in her disheveled clothes, while Chaudhuri's son stood there taunting her about the number of people she had slept with while trying to act coy with him.

The anger at both of them being abandoned at birth, his own accumulated insults, taunts, humiliations, beatings, leftover food, denial of food, denial of rest, discarded clothes, backbreaking work, inhuman living conditions- day after day, year after year, coupled with the present plight of the only person who had ever loved him and who had been given a devastating illness by those who exploited her, erupted like a volcano in his mind. The fight was over in a few minutes. Chaudhuri's semi-conscious son was thrown in a gutter nearby.

They packed quickly, told their neighbours that they were going for a performance and left the city. At the railway station, the ever caring Putli Bai gave some money to the two musicians and asked them to go elsewhere.

✻ ✻ ✻

Two years passed. Their kotha stood desolate, a lock hanging on the door. Its walls developed cracks and peepal trees started growing in the cracks, widening them further. The paint on the doors started peeling, several window-panes were broken and the house gathered dust.

✻ ✻ ✻

I had gone to Mandu for a medical conference. A friend from that area was taking me around.

As we walked around, he pointed to what was believed to

be Rani Rupmati's pavilion, from where she used to see her beloved river Narmada and perhaps had watched Raja Baj Bahadur go to war, never to return.

There was a small crowd around the pavilion. I was surprised to see Bahetu there. I wanted to talk to him and ask him so many questions, but kept quiet- waiting for a moment when I could find him alone. He was wearing very dirty clothes. He was leaning forward and looked very tired. If he recognized me, he showed no signs. He was sitting there looking blankly in the direction of the forest far away, holding the flute in his hands, its shine visible only where his fingers covered the holes.

I heard someone request him to play his flute. Almost mechanically, he put his flute on his lips, closed his eyes and out flowed the song:

"O' beloved, I beseech you.

Do not take the path through the ravine and the river."

Listening to the perfection of the music and the sweet melody, the crowd around him swelled and listened to him in complete silence. They applauded most enthusiastically when he finished and clamoured for more, offering him money. He showed no interest in collecting the money from the outstretched hands. One of the onlookers went around, collected the money and put it in Bahetu's pocket. Bahetu just continued to stare blankly in the direction of Narmada beyond the forest.

As the requests for at least one more song multiplied, he lifted the flute to his lips again. Soon the atmosphere was filled with the sweet strands of the tunes of the famous song:

"Come.

Come back to me, my soul-mate,

My songs beckon you.

My music has fallen silent.."

As the people were lost in the mesmerizing music, he stopped midway and started coughing violently. He got up, went to a corner, leaned against the parapet and spat blood. He started to leave, refusing the money people were trying to offer him.

"His wife died recently. She was very ill', whispered one of the persons selling some trinkets.

While negotiating the steps he stumbled and rolled down. His flute fell from his hands and rolled away. People assembled around him. I leaned and felt for his pulse. And did not find any.

15

The Rat

There was only a primary school near the village. All the boys of rich farmers from the village used to travel to the neighbouring city, once they finished their primary education. There was a very convenient train which, after usual delays, left the station near the village around nine in the morning. The train from the city was supposed to leave by five in the evening, though it hardly ever left before six or even seven. It catered to boys starting from sixth standard till the time they passed matric or intermediate examinations or till their graduation. And of course the rule of being a student was that you never bought a ticket. The station was located almost at the centre of six or seven small villages.

The boys taking that train to the city, loved the situation. It gave them so much more time to be away from home and the constant bickering of their parents. It also gave them so much extra time to ogle the girls and pass lewd comments at them at the city railway station, gossip, smoke cigarettes, rag the new students, tell jokes to each other and boast about how they had harassed their teachers or copied in the examinations and be boisterous in general.

The parents of girls knew the perils of sending girls so far away for education and being away from home for so long. One came to know of harassment, stalking, teasing, kidnapping and even rape of girls and women of all ages so often. Not that they were safe in the village, but they were at least near their parents at all times. Thus the education of the girls from the villages around the railway station stopped after class five. After all, they were only expected to cook and do household and agricultural jobs after marriage. What was the use of education for them?

Pushpa was the daughter of the village priest. And like all the girls of the village, she had completed her education till class five. And after that she stayed home with her mother.

They had no land of their own and they lived on alms-collected by the priest from the village. The priest got up in the morning and after bathing in the river which flowed across the trail to the railway station, sat down to perform his daily puja. And then he picked up his bag, which was essentially a large sheet of rough cloth whose four ends were tied into two knots, making a sort of a bag with a large opening, which he could sling on his shoulders. He went from house to house, being careful not to go to the same area more than once in a fortnight. People would greet him, be blessed by him and offer him "seedha". It was normally some flour, dal, rice, and salt, and very occasionally, one or two potatoes. Even though it was offered to him on a thali, he would open the mouth of his bag and people poured it all together into it. Possibly this practice was a throwback to a time when Buddhist monks went from door to door seeking alms and mixing and mashing all the food before eating- to avoid developing a taste for good food or relishing it. Once the priest had enough for the day he returned home.

Upon his return, his wife and daughter took a sieve and first separated flour from the rice and the dal. And if they did not want to cook "khichadi" (where rice and dal are mixed and cooked), Puspa sat and separated rice from the dal, grain by grain. In earlier days, salt used to come as large crystals and one could separate it from other things, though the smaller pieces almost always got lost in the flour or the rice and the dal. Pushpa had become used to eating food, salted to uncontrolled and varying extents, where corrections could be made only if the salt was less than necessary.

Once in a while the priest was invited to perform Satyanarayan Puja or some ceremony at the homes of his jajmans (adherents or followers). On those occasions he was expected to eat there. However, he had to cook his own food. This used to be an elaborate affair. A place outside the house was cleaned and sprinkled with water. The priest would be given pans-which he washed again, dry twigs of mango and seedha in a large thali. He would put a few bricks together, prepare a make-shift chulha (oven) and start a fire to cooking dal and rice. He would make thick chapattis. He would offer the food to gods and send some of it to the house where everyone took a small morsel with reverence. And then he ate.

While leaving he was given one and a quarter of a rupee as "dakshina" (parting gift or offering) and some seedha for the family. On very special occasions like marriages or birth of a son, really rich farmers gave him a dhoti or even a sari for his wife. People also consulted him to know the date and time of festivals and auspicious time for various works and offered him some grain as fees.

Pushpa had stayed home for two years and revolted. She did not want to be like her mother for the rest of her life-separating flour from rice and dal and eating salted chapattis. She had been a good student. She made her mother beg the women whose sons had passed the higher classes for their books. She read them by herself, following some, not following some and getting very confident that higher education was not difficult. A row lasting several days, several fasts lasting several days, tears, entreaties and persuasions ultimately melted the priest's heart and he travelled with her to the city one day and got her admitted to the school for girls. As she was the only girl going to the school from that station, she sat alone at one of the benches and waited for the train oblivious to all the commotion taking place around her and used the time to study.

Three years passed. She was in ninth standard now. She had won a scholarship and had started to wear decent and reasonable clothes. She had the usual good looks common to upper class Brahmins. She requested her parents to ignore the taunts that they were living on the money made by their daughter and behave as if nothing had changed, hoping to assuage the egos of the nasty villagers. Unfortunately it had the opposite effect as they "concluded" that the priest and his family were play-acting.

❋ ❋ ❋

Manoj was a sickly child. He had suffered from small pox when he was very young and then typhoid. He was small for his age. However he was good at studies- being encouraged by his mother to study hard so that the weakness of his body was of no consequence. Thus while other students often repeated classes he continued to pass every class with good marks and was soon ready to go to the city for education.

His mother was very hesitant. His father lived and worked far away in Bombay. She managed their small land holding with the help of her ageing in-laws. She worried that Manoj would get lost in the crowded city. She worried that he would not be able to board the train or to get off in time when it was crowded. She worried that he would get into a bad company and develop a bad habit. However, Manoj wanted to study and somehow the two convinced each other that it was safe enough for him to go to school in the city. His grandfather took him to the city and got him admitted to the school.

Next day when he reached the station, he was immediately surrounded by many boys out to bully him. They looked at him closely. One of them asked him to spell rat. He replied R, A, T, rat- rat means "Chuha" (the Hindi word for rat). They all laughed loudly and told him that he would be called "Rat" from that day. So they would tell him: Rat do this, Rat do that, Rat go and get a cigarette, Rat carry this bag, Rat come here, and so on.

He would reach the station and try to keep out of their sight. Whenever they got hold of him, they asked him difficult questions for his age and when he failed to answer, they asked him to hold his ears and to do sit-ups till his legs shook with fatigue and pain. They made fun of his physique and asked him to do push-ups till he collapsed with exhaustion. They often asked him to "turn into a murga (cock)". For this, he had to bend low, hold his ears through his legs and raise his buttocks up. After sometime his legs would start shaking with pain. They waited for him to collapse with fatigue and pain and burst into laughter. He quietly obeyed, knowing fully well that they would slap him, kick him, abuse him and insult him in various ways, if he refused.

He never told anything about it to his mother. He also knew that she could not have helped him and it would have only saddened her at being so helpless against rowdies. She was also likely to stop his going to school. Even though it was almost a daily occurrence, he hoped that the compliance would slowly soften them. Perhaps they would even get bored from the monotony of ragging him regularly and find some other target, perhaps in the coming years.

Pushpa used to watch him from a distance, where she sat studying. One day- as he passed by her, she called him. Manoj saw her every day. Even though still quite young, he knew what kind of comments the boys passed about her. He had also heard that she was a very good student and that she had won a scholarship for higher education. He looked around to ascertain if she was really talking to him and not to someone else. Still uncertain, he stopped and asked, with bowed head, "Me?"

She replied "Yes", called him near her and asked him his name, his father's name and the class he was studying. There was a kind of soothing, reassuring quality in her voice that Manoj lost his hesitation and shyness and slowly opened up. She asked him about his favourite subjects and why he liked them, etc. He realised that in all this, sufficient time had passed and the train had arrived. And he also realised that for the first time in three months, he had escaped bullying by the older boys. Pushpa got into the compartment for women.

As soon as he boarded the train, the boys surrounded him

and started asking him what Pushpa had told him. Even though he felt that he was breaking a sacred trust, he told them all for fear of being humiliated again. They all sighed that he had talked to a girl who did not care to even look at them!

Days passed. Every now and then Pushpa called him, asked him about his studies, gave him some suggestions and helped him with some questions. The bullies sighed and plotted a revenge for completely ignoring them and being so nice to Rat. One of them wrote a love letter to Pushpa and asked Manoj to give it to her, telling him that he would be watching him. Manoj took it to Pushpa and gave it to her with shaking hands. He whispered to her to keep it and forgive him. She looked at it and kept it. Later she tore it up into pieces, of course without reading

The city was about twenty kilometres away. Pushpa had to walk back about a kilometre along the track to reach her village across the river.

Both Manoj and Pushpa were concentrating on their studies and forthcoming examinations. Pushpa often called him now to her and helped him with his questions. Manoj had never known the affection of an elder sister and started calling her "Didi" (a term of endearment for an elder sister).

When the boys came to know that he had started calling her Didi, they started calling him "sala" (wife's bother, also used as an abusive term), telling that they were going to make Pushpa their "wife" before long. Manoj thought that it was just a vulgar joke- like all the abusive and vulgar jokes that the boys indulged in and ignored it.

The train from the city got very late that day. The boys

decided to implement a plan which they had discussed often. While they were still discussing, one of them saw Manoj walk past them to the bookshop where he often stood, reading the names of the books and occasionally reading some magazines, if there was no crowd.

The boys called him and forced him to sit with them as a precaution against any leakage of their plan. He was told not to move away from them to avoid being severely thrashed. He sat there, scared. He heard that the boys planned to catch hold of Pushpa on her way to her village from the railway station and have their fun- taking advantage of the darkness. They laughed loudly at their own descriptions of how they were to act out their roles- like who would pin her down, who would cover her mouth to stop her from screaming, laughing loudly at their own bravado. They even held a lottery to decide who would have the first go.

Oblivious to all this, Pushpa sat under a lamp and prepared for her examinations.

The train ultimately arrived at around eight pm. Manoj had been forced to sit with the boys. He desperately wanted to warn her. He even considered shouting out to her even at the risk of being thrashed. However, she was at the other end of the platform and the boys surrounding him did not allow him even to go to toilet.

He was made to walk with them to a compartment. He discreetly noted the location of the compartment for women which Pushpa boarded. The train started and picked up speed. The boys relaxed their vigil over him. They laughed and one of them told him, "So you see Rat, we will make Pushpa our wife today and then you will really be our "sala!" Manoj winced and they all laughed loudly again.

After a few minutes Manoj requested them for a permission to go to toilet. The boys- now confident that the train had picked up speed and he could not escape to warn Pushpa, consented and continued with their nonstop vulgar jokes. He went to the toilet. A little later he emerged and looked out of the window. It was pitch dark.

He opened the gate very quietly and with a great difficulty caught hold of the rods fixed across the widow of the toilet on the outer side of the compartment- first with one hand and then with both. And then he swung out. The toilet was at one end of the compartment and he reached out and crossing the joining area between two compartments, he somehow managed to enter the next compartment in a similar manner. He ran across and swung across the next compartment again and entered the women's compartment. He ran to Pushpa and told her. He whispered that he had to get back quickly to avoid suspicion.

Before Pushpa could react, he slithered back and struggling again and almost falling off the train reached the compartment he had been sitting originally. His shirt and the half-pant had become dirty. One of the boys looked at him with suspicion. Manoj held his stomach with his hands as if he was having a severe cramp. He shifted to a corner away from them and leaning forward, continued to groan every now and then.

The train was now approaching Pushpa's village along the railway track. Soon they would reach the railway bridge and then the railway station. One of the boys remarked that he was already getting excited at the thought of holding Pushpa in his arms.

Manoj felt the train slow down. The steam engine whistled in agony several times and stopped a little ahead of the bridge on the river with a jolt. Someone had pulled the alarm chain. The passengers grumbled that they were getting even further delayed. From the corner of his eyes Manoj, who was still bending low to act out his stomach cramps, saw Pushpa cross the tall grass along the tracks and proceed hurriedly to the houses. He sighed in relief.

One of the boys leaned out of the door and realized that their prey had escaped the elaborate trap that they had prepared. Then he looked closely at Manoj and noticed his dirty shirt and half-pant.

They slapped him. They kicked him. They took their shoes and sandals out and thrashed him. They used their belts to beat him mercilessly, cursing him loudly. When an onlooker overcame the natural reluctance of onlookers to stay away from trouble and tried to intervene, he got thrashed too. The rest of the people in the compartment kept quiet.

Manoj, however, did not cry or plead for mercy. He fainted. As the train stopped at station, the boys carried him out, dumped him on the railway track along with his school bag and fled.

Manoj did not know how long he had been unconscious. When he opened his eyes he found his mother, his grandparents, Pushpa, her parents and some other villagers leaning over his face, holding a lantern. His mother and Pushpa were crying hysterically.

He saw relief in their eyes and blinked. He tried to lift his hand to shield his eyes from the light and screamed in pain. He moved his eyes away from the bright light. He smiled weakly and closed his eyes again- now secure in the belief that Pushpa was in safe hands, at least for now.

16

Trapped in a Metropolis : Jackals of Salt Lake

Arjuna, while pleading for avoidance of war in Gita, worried about the birth of "varna-sankars" or persons of mixed races or mixed"colours" or mixedcastes, following wars. Jean M. Auel wrote several delightful books under the series, "Earth's Children", exploring the encounter of early modern men and Neanderthals. Rudyard Kipling went on to develop a character in a short story to almost a cult status when he introduced Mowgli, a boy brought-up by a wolf in his masterpiece, the Jungle Book. And who can forget the story of Buck, the St. Bernard-Scotch Colie dog of "Call of the wild", going on to father a breed of wolves with an interesting streak in their fur and its sequel, White Fang, the story of domestication of one of them, narrated by the great story teller, Jack London.

But I am going to narrate a simple and sad tale of our wild animals trapped in a metropolis. Passage of time changes the meaning of words. Metropolis originally meant, "The mother city", which sent out settlers; but now it simply stands for a large and busy city. And we shall use it in that sense.

And we shall talk of Calcutta or Kolkata, as one is supposed to call it. While this land mass must have existed for ever, its more modern history started with the landing of Job Charnock at one of the ghats at Sutanati, fortified with a permission from the Emperor Aurangjeb, on August 24, 1690 according to his note in his "Chuttanutty Diary". I do not have courage to go against the courts which have decided a markedly more ancient history of the city!

Our institute started, much later in a distant suburb of Calcutta in the late nineteen sixties. The area was known as Salt Lake. Earlier it was simply known as "The Maath" or "The Field". Bimal Mitra would have us believe that Lord Clive and "Begum Mary Biswas" saw it from the roof of his Kothi at Dumdum. Amitav Ghosh tells us of the pilot whales getting blown into that area during the great cyclone of 1737. The term cyclone itself was to be coined much later by Henry Piddington in 1848, though.

Later in 1741, the bargis (marathas) invaded Kolkata perhaps from the direction of the same Maath. Fifteen years later Nawab Sirajuddaulla invaded Calcutta in June 1756 and renamed it as Alinagar and British historians damned him forever by stamping the word "black-hole" against his name. His army had stayed in The Maath, and our own Nirad Chouaduri, visited it while writing about it in "Clive of India: A Political and Psychological Essay".

The jackals of Salt Lake had seen it all and survived it all, even thriving with famines, murders, riots, and outgrown vegetation. The oldest picture of our institute shows a vast field covered with "kaans" grass, bushes of ber (Indian Plum or Ziziphus Mauritiana), and trees of wild palms, figs, and jungle jalebi (Pithecellobium Dulche). There were several small ponds with fish in them, mongoose, snakes, and a huge swarm of mosquitoes. A large variety by birds; parrots, bulbuls, weaver-birds, golden orioles, sunbirds, sparrows, mynahs, jungle babblers, etc. lived there throughout the year. The neighbouring Kestopur Canal used to be covered by migratory birds during winter. And we reached the site by crossing it with a ferry from the VIP Road.

One of the first structures to come up there was a high brick boundary wall covering about half of the area and a chain link fence for the remaining part. And there was just one gate, continuously manned. This sealed the fate of the jackals which were trapped forever within the boundary walls. What follows, is just a story of their struggle for adoption over decades of living within these walls, with their shrinking habitat, with their changing food habits and even becoming almost diurnal from nocturnal in their life-styles. The birds flew in and out and ultimately moved away as bushes and shrubs were cleared, and the snakes slithered away, but the jackals could not leave.

And now they were two classes of jackals, one which were stuck inside the boundary walls and the others which still roamed the Salt Lake area and beyond and lived along the Kestopur Canal. As evening approached they started their calls and counter-calls which went somewhat as, "hua, hua, hua, hukki, hua, hua", which have filled the Indian forests and country-side for millennia. A call would start from where we now have the Central Park, it would be picked up by the jackals living around the green belt along the Kestopur canal and then it would be followed by the jackals inside the institute. Recall that in eastern UP jackals are called Paharua, as they give out their calls every "prahar" (about three hours) during the night.

As the night descended, they would come out from their holes and play in the sand brought in for construction. There were enough wild birds and small animals for them to survive and they did. The institute expanded, more buildings were needed and more people joined. Stray dogs moved in and have stayed since then. The dogs would bark through the night at the sight of them and chase them, losing them in the growth still covering the unbuilt areas. A cafeteria came up and produced enough trash for them and they survived.

Slowly they started becoming a little more adventurous and came out even before it was too dark, at least during the week- ends when there were not many people. They maintained their distance from the dogs and people, the dogs chasing them on sight. We had planted some fast growing trees like Casuarina and Eucalyptus. The ber bushes also prospered and gave patches of thick foliage for them to live and hunt.

When a patch had to be cleared they started living close to the garage where our drivers stayed during the night shifts and who often found them moving near their retiring rooms. The drivers would throw some food at them and slowly they were less scared of them. The dogs still chased them and barked at them from a distance.

Perhaps it started it with the pups but no one is sure. The pups would, during the nights, approach the guards at the gate and happily "smiling", approach even the dogs and play with them. After some initial hostility the dogs too started playing with the pups and slowly stopped chasing the jackals when they came out during the nights. The jackals were still nocturnal.

As Salt Lake area got more populated, the jackals outside the fenced-in area started moving away. We also moved into the campus of our institute by then and on the nights when I was up reading or working, I would see the jackals come out from the foliage, chase a rat or a mole, look into the trash-cans, and play in the sand, some-times digging up the ground to the annoyance of the gardener. Our gates were always manned and the jackals looked in that direction with soul-full eyes never daring to approach the gate with the watchmen with their sticks and a number of stray dogs which give them company during the long nights. It was then that we noticed that the calls of the jackals during the night were becoming less and less frequent, coming hardly once a week- even though still answered by the jackals, which were fenced in. It was not difficult for us to know that not only the calls were fewer and far in between, even the number of jackals participating in the "chorus" was perceptibly decreasing. We have not heard these calls for long. And strangely enough, the jackals trapped inside also do not give a call any more.

Some years ago I started noticing, especially when I went to the institute on weekends or when I worked till very late, that the jackals which were still left, appeared even before the sun-set and they were given a "friendly chase" by the dogs; the jackals not running fast enough and the dogs not making any serious attempt to catch up and attack them, and definitely not barking.

And now since early last year we have started noticing some "dog-jackals" which come out of the very little foliage which is still left in the institute, a little before the sun sets. They are still rather shy and still keep a safe distance from people but do not hide from them and sometimes they are seen moving with the dogs. Their fur is not as rich and shiny as those of jackals which are normally black on the back, golden on the sides, and white in the belly region. Their tails do not have longer fur and they often hold it horizontally and straight.

Now they are trapped forever in this metropolis. The chase in the wild, the call every three hours, the hunting in pairs, the eating frenzy after the kill of a wild animal or on finding a carcass, are all forgotten as they learn to survive. Will their progeny, after a few more generations, retain any of the traits of their ancestors, which must have dominated the landscape of Calcutta at one time as the names like Baghmari ("tiger-killed") and Sealdah ("pond of the jackal") are to be believed.

Yes, Arjuna, you were right, this war between urbanization and wilderness has given rise to a "varna-sankar" of dogs and jackals which are neither dogs nor jackals and which neither bark nor give a call and yet they do not fully trust either men or dogs.

17

The Silent Whisper

Grandma lay in bed, in the little hut outside the main house. It was dark. It was raining. It was lonely. The thatched roof of the outhouse leaked at some places and the two cows continuously shifted their positions to escape from the rainwater dripping on them. Yes, the roof should have been repaired during the summer. For whom, she wondered?

Her elder son had migrated to the city in the south, with his wife and children. After all, what was there in the village for him? Snakes, scorpions, mud, dust, kerosene lamps, and a well whose water bred worms and dysentery, a house having walls of mud and a village ruled by jealousy, theft, robbery, fights and murders?

He had wanted a better future for his children. Yes, it was better that they lived in the city. It did not matter that the house where they lived was near a canal of dirty, stinking water which carried all the filth of the city. It did not matter that they cooked food on coal taken from railway engines, which smelled of sulphur. It did not matter that one could hardly breathe when they started the coal-oven which belched out smoke to envelop the entire neighbourhood.

It did not matter that they did not get fresh twigs of neem to brush their teeth and could not afford milk and had to buy mangoes and could hardly afford vegetables. The creepers of pumpkin and gourds in front of her house produced a huge amount of vegetables. During winter there were potatoes and peas and gram, even though she was not able to look after the fields well. It did not matter that her grandchildren ate chapattis of rotten wheat from the ration shop, without any coating of ghee; in fact they could not put ghee even in the dal.

The last of the mangoes were still around and as wind picked up she could hear them dropping from the trees. She could make out the location of their fall, from the sound they made. If her grandchildren were home, she could have delighted them by guessing their location. But they were not there.

Still, she would try to collect them in the morning, more as a matter of habit, though she would not be able to eat them. She knew very well that mangoes were very expensive in the city and her younger son was so fond of ripe mangoes.

She thought of the school in the city. The children there sat on a chair and had a table, there was a proper school building and it had teachers for all the classes, and the children had to have a neat uniform. The school in the village was held under a tree, there was only one teacher for the entire primary school. He mostly worked in his own fields and asked one of the grownup kids to `mind the classes'. Sometimes he called the entire school to work on the field, bashing those who refused to work for him.

Yes, it was good that her grandchildren were studying in city, even if she found it increasingly difficult to communicate with them when they came for a visit, as they slowly adopted the dialect of the city. Yes, she knew that other children looked down upon them as they were poor and spoke in the dialect of the rustics.

Soon, her thoughts were drifting again. Did she have a fever? She did shiver once in a while. It must be the rain and the cool breeze, she thought and wrapped the thick sheet around her. The rain turned into a drizzle and stopped. The wind picked up and blew the clouds away. A yellowing moon peeped from behind the clouds. A jackal howled in the distance. A little later, several of its tribe picked up the refrain.

Her dog, lying nearby became alert and then realizing that they were far away, dozed off again. From her cot, she could see a fox scampering for food. The fox was not big enough for the dog to worry.

It must be hungry, it had been raining intermittently for some days. An owl hooted and a bat flew by. Not long ago, several flying foxes had lived in the orchard, they were all gone, like the monkeys, like the wolves, like the peacocks, like her younger son. And she too dozed off.

And then the moon went down. The sky was almost clear now, the stars could be seen. She woke with a start from her recurring dream and could see the large cluster of colourful twinkling stars, called `kach-bachia'. Morning was not too far, she thought. And then the Venus came up, shining brilliantly. She was fully awake, well before the eastern horizon turned pink. Yet she could not forget the recurring dream about her younger son, which had bothered her every night. And she had never been able to see the end of the dream, she always awoke just before the end.

Her younger son was a source of joy to her. He was full of life and laughter, a very good athlete, and fond of tricks. She had worked hard to put him in a college. He was also a very good hockey player.

Once a month he came home, bringing with him shining cups from the matches he had won. And he told her stories of distant cities where he was often going to play. She heard that he was likely to be selected for the state or even the national team. She could not imagine what it meant and prayed to protect him from the evil eye.

One day someone had told her that he was seen giving a speech at a mill in the city where the workers were on strike. Yes, she knew he was always talking about low wages being paid to workers, about their extremely bad living conditions, about the high rate of interest being charged by the money-lender and the landlord of the village and about corruption in general. He was also talking of distant lands where there was no poverty and no disease.

She was always telling him not to worry about the problem of others. And yet deep in her heart she liked to hear him talk of these things. He was so different from her elder son! The elder son went to work in the neighbouring town, came back every day, taught his children, and kept to himself. He was always keeping away from trouble, any kind of trouble. He had a family to look after, he always told.

Then one day her elder son had brought a newspaper with a picture of her younger son. He was stopping a policeman from hitting a man on the road. And there were other policemen who were hitting her son. The anger of the policemen at being stopped could be seen clearly. She was scared, very scared. And surprisingly she could feel the force of contempt in the look of her son. He did not come home that month.

And after that every once in a while someone would bring news of his joining some group or other of young men protesting against something or other. Her elder son was often grumbling at being questioned about his brother by people whom he did not know and who were perhaps policemen in civilian clothes or informers. She would sit and worry and imagine him playing games, telling jokes, playing with his nephews, and laughing. She always remembered him as laughing. And yet she always worried. May gods protect him from the evil-eye, she would say.

Several months later he came. He did not bring any cups. He looked lean, tanned, and very exhausted. His palms were much rougher than before. He was also very silent and replied to her questions in monosyllables. He even did not reply to her question about a large scar on his belly. And he stayed for several days, keeping mostly indoors. Her elder son maintained a stony silence.

And then, one night she woke up to find her younger son missing. She heard some whispers and followed the sound to see him talking to some strangers. She kept quiet. In the morning four young men came to her house. Her son took her aside and told that they would stay for a few days.

By noon a truckload of gun-toting policemen with an officer in a jeep surrounded her house. Things had moved quickly. Her younger son had come out and told that they would surrender. She was confused. She did not know what was happening. Her elder son had kept quiet and the entire village had become devoid of people. The strangers and her younger son had assembled in the courtyard. They had no weapons. They were taken to the truck and it drove off. No one told her a thing, as if she did not exist.

That was the lost she saw him.

The memories of the next several days were very blurred in her mind. She only remembered that her elder son had migrated to the city in the south soon after, leaving her alone. And she remembered that people became silent when she approached.

And ever since she had slept in the little hut outside the house. And ever since she had a recurring dream. She would dream that her younger son and his friends were being taken to the ravine and they were being dragged to the edge.

And then the police officer was aiming the gun at them. And then she would awaken.

And ever since, when she closed her eyes- she would see the enactment of this scene, till the aiming of the guns. And then her mind would stop, refusing to imagine beyond this, refusing to recall beyond this.

She had once walked to the place where the `encounter' had taken place. She remembered every detail of the terrain, the boulders, the acacia trees, the pits. She remembered the clothes her son wore when the police took him. She had stood there and seen in her mind's eye- seen her son being dragged, seen his clothes being torn, seen the police officer aiming the gun at his head.

She could recall every step of her walk, at will, and yet her mind refused to imagine what happened next. However, once in a while she heard a whisper, a whisper coming to her from across the mists of her memories.

The police officer had said something to her elder son and had smiled. The policemen had laughed- crudely, as only policemen do.

And yet her mind had always refused to decipher the whisper. She only remembered that her elder son, my father, had never looked into her eyes again.

www.ingramcontent.com/pod-product-compliance
Lightning Source LLC
Chambersburg PA
CBHW050821180626

46814CB00004B/1396